P9-CCW-285

THE CASE OF THE
BUG
ON THE
RUN

The First Kids Mysteries

The Case of the Rock 'n' Roll Dog
The Case of the Diamond Dog Collar
The Case of the Ruby Slippers
The Case of the Piggy Bank Thief
The Case of the Missing Dinosaur Egg

THE CASE OF THE
BUG
ON THE
RUN

MARTHA FREEMAN

Holiday House / New York

Printed and bound in July 2013 at Maple Press, York, PA USA
First Edition
1 3 5 7 9 10 8 6 4 2
www.holidayhouse.com
Library of Congress Cataloging-in-Publication Data

Freeman, Martha, 1956–
The case of the bug on the run / by Martha Freeman. — First edition.
pages cm — (First kids mystery ; #6)
Summary: When their pet cockroach disappears and then reappears wearing a tiny
transmitter, seven-year-old Tessa and ten-year-old Cammie, daughters of the first
female president, search for spies in the White House.
ISBN 978-0-8234-2872-4 (hardcover)
1. White House (Washington, D.C.)—Juvenile fiction. [1. White House (Washington, D.C.)—
Fiction.   2. Presidents—Family—Fiction.   3. Sisters—Fiction.   4. Cockroaches—
Fiction.   5. Pets—Fiction.   6. Spies—Fiction.   7. Washington (D.C.)—Fiction.
8. Mystery and detective stories.]   I. Title.
PZ7.F87496Cak 2013
[Fic]—dc23
2013009191

For the real Mr. Dustin Brackbill, librarian at Mt. Nittany Elementary School.

And with thanks to Linda Margusity, Kimber Hershberger and their third graders, for lending expertise and bugs.

CHAPTER ONE

Cockroaches have lived on Earth for 350 million years. They survived the asteroid crash that killed the dinosaurs. They survived the freezing-cold Ice Ages. Every day, they survive about a zillion cans of bug spray.

Cockroaches are tough.

But that does not make them popular.

Listen to this: *"Ewwwww!"*

That's most people's opinion about our new pet, which happens to be a giant Madagascar hissing cockroach. My sister, Tessa, and I brought him home from the National Zoo in a disk-shaped plastic box.

Not just anyone can adopt a pet from the National Zoo. Tessa and I are lucky. We are plain, ordinary American kids, but our mom is president of the United States. This gives us some unusual privileges. Besides adopting cockroaches, we get to fly on a special air force jet when we go on vacation. And we get to live in a big house with elevators and its own movie theater—the White House.

It was a Tuesday in July, one of the only weeks of the whole summer when we didn't have camp or away-from-home vacation. We were in our bedroom, which is on the second floor over the North Portico, also known as the front door. We had let our pet cockroach out of the plastic box and Tessa was holding him. Mr. Ross, who's in charge of the White House staff, was showing us and our grandmother the tank where the cockroach would live. It used to be a fish tank. One of the White House carpenters had made a lid for the top.

Granny said, "Tell me again, girls. Why is it you wanted a cockroach?"

I said, "It was Tessa's idea."

Tessa said, "The zoo had an extra. I thought maybe they would send him to live on a farm in the country. But then the keeper said not exactly, and I got a bad, bad feeling. So what could I do?" She waved her arms the way she does. "Someone had to save him!"

My little sister is a drama queen. She is also famous for liking things no one else likes. Compared to some of her favorites—like sea slugs, naked mole rats and squids—this cockroach wasn't bad. Picture an orange-striped wide-body beetle with a black helmet, spiky black legs and two delicate, curious antennae.

Smiling, Tessa held the cockroach out to Granny and Mr. Ross. "You can hold him if you want."

The cockroach hissed.

Tessa grinned like a proud parent. "Isn't that amazing? They're the only insect that can do that! But maybe I better put him back. You can have a turn next time."

There was a layer of dirt, twigs and leaves at the bottom of the tank. Gently, Tessa set the bug down and replaced the lid. The bug went exploring.

At the same time, all six Ks strolled over to take a look.

The Ks are the stray kittens we found under a bush last spring. Tessa and I were supposed to give them away to good homes, but now we're hoping maybe Granny will forget.

The cockroach's tank was on the low table by the little sofa. One by one, all six kittens jumped up on the table, sat down and stared at our new pet through the glass. Their tails were swishing.

"To a critter of the feline persuasion," said Mr. Ross, "that cockroach must look like a chewier, crunchier rodent."

Tessa looked horrified. "They can't get in, can they?"

Mr. Ross shook his head. "No way, no how. And your bug can't get out, either. With these hooks on the lid, this tank is guaranteed escape-proof."

Granny crossed her arms over her chest. "It better be."

CHAPTER TWO

We had spent most of the morning at the zoo. Now it was time for lunch. We would be eating in the third-nicest dining room in the White House, the one on the second floor, which is where we mostly live. In the second-floor dining room, we would sit at a table for twelve set with a white cloth. The food would come from the White House kitchen downstairs. It would be served on china plates by a butler.

Don't think we always eat this way.

A lot of the time, if it's just our family, we sit at the table in our own kitchen and serve ourselves. Sometimes Granny even cooks. But that week we had a lot of houseguests:

First, there were the Veritys, who live in Beverly Hills, California—mom Kendall, dad Ruben, and daughter Lily. Lily just turned four. She looks a little like my sister—blond and cute. She thinks seven-year-old Tessa is like a goddess or something.

Besides the Verity family, there was Kirk Schott, who is an engineer and used to be in the air force with my dad. He lives in California, too.

The next guest, you've probably seen on TV: Amaro Amaro, the chef. He had just arrived that morning. In case you don't know, he's the one who's famous for making vegetables taste yummy and for wearing wrap-around glasses and spangled bandannas.

The Veritys, Mr. Schott and Mr. Amaro were staying with us for a few days. The White House has 132 rooms, so there's plenty of space for sleepover guests. The last guest who joined us for lunch that day wasn't staying with us, though. She lives in Washington and goes to my school. Her name is Courtney Lozana, and she's my best friend. She likes to eat with us, especially when celebrities are visiting.

Everyone else at lunch was family: Tessa and Granny, and my aunt Jen and her son, Nate, who is ten and knows everything. Finally, there's me! I'm Cameron Parks, Cammie for short. I am ten years old like Nate, but I don't know everything.

"Totally awesome to be here!" Mr. Amaro looked around at the crystal chandelier, the oil paintings, and the flower arrangements on the table and sideboard. He had just arrived at the White House that morning. "What's for chow?"

"Chicken salad, I believe," said Aunt Jen. "And it's awesome to meet you as well."

After introductions, we all sat down. "Mr. Amaro is

speaking tonight at a dinner for school nutritionists," Aunt Jen explained. "The idea is to encourage healthy eating."

Mr. Amaro slapped his knee. "School nutritionists, my foot—they're lunch ladies, is what they are!"

All of us kids giggled.

Aunt Jen smiled politely, then turned to Mr. Schott. "And how are your meetings going, Kirk?"

"Very well, thank you for asking," said Mr. Schott. My parents say Mr. Schott is nice, but to me he always seems serious and a little stuck-up. Today he was wearing a suit, while everyone else had on casual summer clothes.

"Now, say again, Kirk, what it is you're doing. I can't quite get my brain around it," said Mr. Verity.

"I'm afraid the details are—*ahem*—top secret," said Mr. Schott, "but it has to do with miniaturized drone technology. I am something of an authority."

Nate said, "A drone is a little airplane that flies without a pilot—in case anybody was wondering."

"Why do airplanes want to do that?" Tessa asked.

Mr. Schott explained, "Well, for example, search-and-rescue teams can send them flying—*ahem*—over cliffs and boulders to find lost persons."

"Also, drones can spy on the enemy!" said Nate.

Mr. Schott frowned.

Courtney looked up. "Seriously? My dad might be interested in that."

Courtney's dad is Alan Lozana. He used to be a TV reporter, and now he has a blog about politics.

"Drones—*ahem*—are not really news, if I may say so," Mr. Schott told Courtney. "They have been operational for many years now."

Courtney said, "Then never mind," and went back to pushing lettuce leaves around her plate.

Granny turned to Mr. Verity. "And what about you, Ruben? Are you having your accustomed business success?"

Mr. Verity flashed his very white teeth. "I'm afraid that's TBD—to be determined. Rome wasn't built in a day, you know, and neither was *Playground Smackdown*."

Mr. Verity is a reality-TV show producer. *Playground Smackdown* is one of his big hits. He knows my mom because a long time ago, he helped her with TV stuff on one of her political campaigns.

"I think there's kind of a TV show going on in Tessa's and my room," I said. Then I explained how the kittens were fascinated by our new pet.

Courtney stopped eating. "Your new pet's a bug? That's disgusting!"

Tessa scowled. "Well, maybe my bug thinks *we're* disgusting. Did you ever think of that?"

Lily echoed, "Skusting!"

Granny raised her eyebrows. "Tessa?"

Tessa shrugged. "Just sayin'."

Mr. Verity shook his head. "You people are too

much! But seriously." He tapped his jaw with his finger. "I'm loving this idea of reality TV for pets. So very LB—low-budget! Plus we've got ready-made theme music—'*La Cucaracha.*' That means 'cockroach,' doesn't it? Hey, Max? Look that up, will you?"

Mr. Verity's phone was next to his plate on the table. Now it blinked, and the face of Max, Mr. Verity's assistant in California, appeared on the screen. "Sure thing, boss."

My grandmother turned to Mr. Schott. "I seem to remember you do research on bugs as well."

Mr. Schott nodded. "Indeed. We study their brains, eyes, ears and skeletons to use as models for robotic structures. I'm—*ahem*—something of an authority on that, too."

Mr. Amaro chimed in. "I have an interest in bugs myself. Did you know people around the world eat grubs, mealworms and crickets?"

Everyone stopped chewing for a moment. I swallowed hard. Then, from Mr. Verity's phone, Max spoke up: "Ick."

Mr. Amaro grinned. "Bugs are cheap and full of protein. Besides which, raising them is easier on the planet than raising chickens and cows. Say you grind up bugs and add them to school lunches—zowie! The nutrition value skyrockets! I have mentioned my idea to President Parks."

Courtney looked up from her lettuce leaves. "Wait—what? You mean President Parks wants American schoolchildren to eat ground-up bugs?"

Uh-oh. Sometimes it's a problem when Courtney tells

her dad stuff and he puts it in his blog. Now Granny and Aunt Jen both started to explain that my mom for sure does not want American schoolchildren eating bugs.

But they never had the chance.

Because all of a sudden, a superstorm blew in.

CHAPTER THREE

It was a fur tornado that came out of nowhere, and it was followed by a fast-slithering snake that shot across the rug, under the table and around the legs of Courtney's chair, where it tangled and caught and yanked and then—before you could say "barbecued cricket"— Courtney tipped over onto Cousin Nate, who tipped over onto Mrs. Verity, who tipped over onto Granny . . .

A chain reaction!

And it would've gone all around the table . . .

. . . except that Granny stuck out her foot and pushed everybody back upright again.

Have I mentioned that Granny works out?

Anyway, all that happened in the single solitary second before Mr. Bryant rushed through the doorway. "Hooligan, there you are! Come back this instant!"

The superstorm was not really a tornado. It was really our big furry mutt, Hooligan. The scary snake was really his leash.

Hooligan suspected he'd done something bad and

hid under the table till Tessa crawled down, hugged him and promised he wasn't in trouble.

Meanwhile, Mr. Bryant apologized. He's our family's friend and also in charge of Hooligan on weekdays. "I turned away to sip my coffee," Mr. Bryant explained, "and off he went. You know he hates to miss a chance for a treat from the table."

By now, our dog was sitting at Mr. Bryant's side and displaying his most noble profile.

Aunt Jen said, "I'm certain no one here would feed the dog from the table"—which must mean she hadn't noticed the mayonnaise on Hooligan's nose.

Mr. Bryant led Hooligan away. Then Granny made sure no one was hurt and Aunt Jen made sure no china was broken. After that, lunch was over.

Tessa and I had just shoved back our chairs when Mr. Schott turned to us. "Would you girls—*ahem*—mind showing me your new pet this afternoon?"

"Cool idea!" said Mr. Verity. "Can we come, too?"

"Give us a couple of minutes," I said, "and we'll bring him out to the Center Hall."

Back in our bedroom, the kittens were still in place, with their tails still swishing. But when Tessa and I looked in the cockroach's tank, we found we had a slight problem.

Our new pet had disappeared.

CHAPTER FOUR

Tessa squealed and waved her arms the way she does. "Mr. Ross was wrong! The cockroach has escaped!"

I sighed. In my family, it's not the boy who cried wolf. It's the little sister.

"I think he's only hiding, Tessa," I said. "Look at the Ks. If the star had left the show, would the audience still be watching?"

We call the kittens the Ks because Granny won't let us give them names. She says their real owners will do that, just as soon as we give them all away. Since they don't have names, we use letters and numbers—OK for Orange Kitten, BK for Black Kitten, and TK 1, 2, 3 and 4 for Tabby Kittens.

By now, Courtney had jumped up on my bed. "If that cockroach so much as touches my toes," she squealed, "I'll have a heart attack, and you can't stop me!"

Tessa and I, meanwhile, knelt by the tank and waited. After a few seconds, some leaves quivered; then two curious antennae and a black helmet surfaced.

The Ks were excited. They meowed and batted the glass. BK even tried to climb inside.

"The rock star has returned!" said Tessa.

"And the fans go wild," I said. "Now, before he decides to hide again, let's take this show on the road."

The Center Hall is like a big room—with white carpeting, a piano and bookcases—that runs the length of the White House's second floor. To get there from our bedroom, you walk out the door, turn left and take five steps.

Tessa carried one end of the tank, and I carried the other. Courtney followed. We set the tank on a table. The Ks paraded in behind us, then resumed their front-row seats.

"Too much!" said Mr. Verity when he came in with Lily. "And those cats—they're like a focus group! Give 'em credit cards, and next thing you're selling catnip and litter boxes! Isn't that right, Max?"

"Absolutely, boss." The phone was now clipped to Mr. Verity's belt.

Meanwhile, Mr. Schott had come in, followed by Charlotte, my favorite Secret Service agent, and then Courtney's dad, Alan Lozana.

"Sorry to intrude," said Mr. Lozana, "but I've come to pick up my daughter for her riding lesson."

I introduced Mr. Verity and Mr. Lozana. "You're a Washington blogger, hunh?" Mr. Verity said. "Max, make a note for a new show, *Washington Blogger*. Tell me, Mr. Lozana. Is your life full of passion, action and humiliation? Viewers love humiliation."

"Absolutely," said Mr. Lozana. "In fact, if you want to send a camera crew to my home . . ."

Courtney chimed in. "Oh, yes, please! And would you also send a wardrobe consultant? My parents are totally embarrassing."

Mr. Verity smiled. "We don't mind dressing our stars up a little, but behavior must be completely natural. It's when people forget about the hidden camera that great television happens."

By now I had figured out a little secret. Mr. Verity proposes a new show to everyone he meets. Most of the time, there's no new show, but Courtney and her dad didn't know that. And right away, the three of them started making plans.

Meanwhile, Mr. Schott had pulled out his phone to take a picture.

Charlotte was posted in the Center Hall that afternoon. "Uh, Mr. Schott?" she said. "I'm sorry, but I can't let you do that inside the White House."

Mr. Schott said, "It's only the insect I'm interested in."

Charlotte shook her head.

Mr. Schott said, "National security. I understand," and put his phone away.

Lily tugged my arm. "Whatsa big bug's name?"

Tessa and I looked at each other. We'd been so busy, we hadn't even given him one! "Do you have a suggestion?" Tessa asked.

Lily thought so hard her face scrunched up. Finally, she said, "Fluffy."

Oh, dear. Fluffy is not a very good name for a

cockroach. But we didn't want to say so and hurt Lily's feelings.

Luckily, Mrs. Hedges, the grumpiest maid in the White House, came out of the Treaty Room at that moment. She was carrying a feather duster.

"Hey, Mrs. Hedges—come and look!" Tessa called. "And don't worry. The zookeeper said cockroaches are pretty clean, I mean for cockroaches."

I had a bright idea. "Lily, would you mind if we gave somebody else a chance to name the cockroach?"

Lily's lip quivered like she might cry. Tessa said quickly, "We could name one of the kittens Fluffy."

This cheered Lily right up. "The black one! She's my fa-vo-wit."

"Okay," I said, "and Mrs. Hedges, would you like to name the cockroach?"

My idea had been that you can't hate something if you name it. And I was right! Mrs. Hedges peered into the tank. "What kind of cockroach did you say he is, again?"

"Madagascan," I said.

"Then what about Madison?" said Mrs. Hedges.

"Madison like James Madison!" said Tessa. "He was the fourth president of the United States and lived in the White House two hundred years ago."

Mrs. Hedges smiled. "James Madison is a fine name."

My family believes children need outdoor recreation no matter how hot and humid Julys are in Washington,

DC. That's why Tessa and I had a full afternoon—tennis lessons, throwing the Frisbee for Hooligan and swimming lessons.

One good thing about our house: we did all those things without ever leaving our big backyard, which is also known as the White House South Lawn.

It was nearly five o'clock when we came in to clean up and get dressed for Mr. Amaro's dinner thing. We knew when we opened our bedroom door we'd find dresses already laid out for us to wear. Anytime we go to an event where we might be photographed, Aunt Jen chooses our clothes. If you think that means she doesn't trust us to pick out our own clothes . . . you got that right.

Anyway, what we didn't know was what else we'd find in our room: a great big mess!

Our new pet's tank was lying on its side on the floor with the lid wide open. Leaves and dirt were strewn all over the carpet. As for our big orange-striped cockroach—there was no sign of him at all.

CHAPTER FIVE

"Cammie, what happened?" said Tessa.

"I don't know, but we'd better clean it up and find James Madison fast," I said. "Otherwise, Granny is going to kill us."

The two of us cleaned and searched at the same time. We looked under the tank, then put it back on the table. We swept up the dirt and looked under every twig and leaf. We looked under the lid, then set it back on the tank and hooked it closed.

"It must be the Ks that knocked it over," said Tessa, "and then James Madison got out and ran away."

"I don't think the Ks are heavy enough," I said. "And wait a sec—where *are* the Ks?" I scanned our bedroom without seeing a single one. "Oh, great. I wonder if they left at the same time the bug did. Maybe someone let them out."

Tessa smiled. "Know what, Cammie? This seems to me like the start of a mystery."

Since we moved into the White House in January,

Tessa, Nate and I have helped solve five mysteries. We've even been on TV! Granny's the one who taught us about detecting. Before she was a judge, she was a police officer.

"I don't think so, Tessa," I said. "I mean, where's the bad guy? No one would steal a cockroach. Come on— James Madison's got to be around here somewhere. Let's keep looking."

I peered under my bed, then Tessa's. I looked under our dressers, then under each of the chairs. I looked in the closet and even in my shoes.

Tessa didn't look anywhere. She just stared at the tank.

"Some help you are," I said.

"I'm thinking!" said Tessa. "If the Ks didn't knock it over, who did?"

I shrugged. "Hooligan, I guess."

"Oka-a-ay," said Tessa. "So say I'm Hooligan." She put her hands up like doggy paws and let her tongue loll out of her mouth. For a blond seven-year-old girl, she looked surprisingly like our big, furry, too-energetic dog.

Then she shoved the tank, and it tipped over. Only it didn't fall onto the floor. It stayed on the table. And the lid didn't come off, either.

Now I was interested. "Okay, so that's not what happened. How about if Hooligan banged into the table and made the whole thing tilt?"

Tessa made her Hooligan face again, dropped down on all fours and—*bam!*—bumped her rear end into the table with too much energy. Sure enough, the table tipped and the tank slid to the rug. Then it rolled once and came to rest upside down.

"Hunh," I said after a second. "If it happened that way, James Madison couldn't have escaped. He wouldn't have had a way out."

"And the dirt didn't spill, either," Tessa said.

"Maybe it wasn't an accident," I said.

"Maybe not." Tessa was excited. "Maybe somebody just wanted it to look like one. And that would be a mystery! You know what I think? The First Kids are back in business!"

"Not right this minute they're not." Charlotte had come in the door behind us. "Because the First Kids are supposed to meet Ms. Major in the State Dining Room for photos." Charlotte spotted the tank on the floor. "What happened?"

"James Madison is gone," I said.

Charlotte frowned. "What about Thomas Jefferson and George Washington? Are they still around?"

"Not President James Madison!" Tessa waved her arms. "The bug James Madison!"

Charlotte pressed a button on her radio. "Hang on while I tell Mr. Ross."

"*No-o-o!*" Tessa whined. "Mr. Ross will get out the bug spray for sure!"

Charlotte muted the radio. "Girls, be real. The White House can't host a formal dinner when there's a foreign cockroach on the loose."

Tessa glared at me. "Cammie, you never should

have told Charlotte! In the end, she's just a grown-up, and she's on the grown-up side."

Charlotte protested. "Hey, no fair. I used to be a kid! I even had a pet iguana that one time ran away and scared the neighbors' dogs."

"Did you get it back?" I asked.

"Yeah, but then Mom sent it to live in a swamp in the country. At least"—Charlotte looked thoughtful—"that's where she told me it went. All right. I won't tell Mr. Ross . . . yet."

I said, "Thank you," and Tessa gave Charlotte a great big hug.

"But hurry and get dressed now!" Charlotte said. "You can look for your pet later. I just hope he doesn't turn up in a salad."

CHAPTER SIX

My sister used to be the kind of girl who took forever to fix herself up for a party. Now that we've gotten so busy solving mysteries, though, she's changed. When necessary, she can get ready as fast as me—which means basically in no time at all.

Don't tell, but that night we didn't even take showers.

Instead, we splashed our faces, pulled on our dresses, foofed our hair and ran down the Grand Staircase to the Entrance Hall. There a hundred lunch ladies and a few lunch gentlemen were eating appetizers and listening to a member of the United States Marine Band play the piano. Mom, wearing a dark blue dress, was in the Cross Hall, shaking hands with party guests. We hadn't seen her all day, and when she saw us, she winked.

The State Dining Room has white walls, gold light fixtures and pink-and-white carpeting. Over the fireplace is a painting of President Lincoln. He isn't wearing his hat, and he's thinking hard about something. The round tables were set for guests, with arrangements of sunflowers in the middle. There was a long table for Mr. Amaro, my mom, Aunt Jen and a few other important people at the front of the room.

We found Ms. Major in a corner with one of the White House photographers.

"I thought we'd have to send out a search party," Ms. Major said when we walked in.

Tessa looked at me. "That's what we need, Cammie—a search party!"

"What is it you're searching for?" Ms. Major asked.

"Nothing!" we both said—even though I was at that moment scanning the rug for any skittering thing that was fat, orange and black. Then Mr. Patel, the cutest White House butler, stuck a tray in front of my face . . . and everything on it was fat, orange and black!

I couldn't help it. I shrieked.

Mr. Patel jumped.

And the tray might have flipped to the floor, except that Mr. Patel is not only cute, but also he can juggle.

"I'm sorry, Cameron," he apologized after he caught his breath. "I didn't know you were scared of carrots."

Tessa looked at the tray. "Those are some funky-looking carrots."

"Carrot croquettes with poppy seeds," Ms. Major explained. "Cammie doesn't have to eat them. But for the sake of the picture, a smile would be better than a look of sheer terror."

I was embarrassed. I actually like carrots. I popped

an appetizer into my mouth. It was sweet and crunchy. Again I prepared to smile for the camera—but this time I truly did see something moving on the floor.

It wasn't a cockroach.

It was a kitten paw!

The tables were set with floor-length white cloths. A wicked little black paw had poked out from beneath one. What was BK—I mean Fluffy—doing here?

The photographer hadn't seen what I had. Now she peered over the top of her camera and sighed. "Puzzled surprise is not an improvement."

I started to apologize for my face, but then I saw a second paw—this one with tabby stripes—and after that the tip of an orange swishing tail. I elbowed Tessa and pointed. Her eyes widened. "Oh, no—if Granny sees the Ks, we'll have to give them away for sure. What do we do, Cammie?"

"Uh . . . be polite, eat our dinner and hope for the best?" I said.

Tessa waved her arms. "Is that supposed to be a plan? Because if it is, it's your lamest one yet!"

CHAPTER SEVEN

Tessa was right. My plan was lame. But for a while, it worked.

The point of the dinner was to get people thinking about kids and healthy eating. So the menu included lots of fruits and vegetables that kids like. Besides carrots, there was a green salad with orange slices, cold strawberry soup, and whole wheat pizza with fresh tomatoes.

Tessa and I sat a table with Nate, Lily, Mrs. Verity and four nice lunch ladies from Pennsylvania. Mr. Verity and Mr. Schott couldn't be there because they had business meetings.

Between dinner and dessert, Mom introduced Mr. Amaro, and he talked for a few minutes about how to add fruits and vegetables to school lunches.

"And in conclusion," he said, "please remember this simple equation: fruits plus vegetables times kids equals awesome!"

One of the lunch ladies at our table raised her hand

to ask a question, but Mr. Amaro wasn't taking any. Instead, he excused himself and left in a hurry.

Then it was time for dessert—some kind of white ice cream with green sprinkles served in a crystal goblet. Mrs. Verity tried it first and announced, "I like it. The parsnips add zip."

By this time, the event was almost over, and I had stopped worrying about the Ks. Probably, I thought, they had run away when all the people came in. Worst case? They were hidden in out-of-the-way corners, asleep.

Too bad I was wrong.

All through dinner, the kittens had been lying in wait for just the right moment to cause complete and utter cat-astrophe!

CHAPTER EIGHT

It's hard to know what goes on in the mind of a kitten. But considering what happened next, I have a guess.

Fluffy, formerly known as BK, was catnapping under a table when she woke up and saw a skinny, dangerous reptile threatening to bite the ankle of a poor innocent lunch gentlemen. What could she do? She pounced!

It wasn't her fault she was wrong about the reptile, which wasn't planning to bite any ankle at all because it wasn't really a reptile. Instead, it was the twisted shape of the gentleman's untied shoelace. Likewise, it wasn't Fluffy's fault that the gentleman never expected a random furball with claws to fasten itself to his foot during a formal White House dinner, so that when it did, he sprang from his chair and kicked like an NFL player—sending Fluffy sailing football-like across the room . . .

. . . to a crash landing in a bowl of sunflowers at the head table.

Yellow petals exploded everywhere and Fluffy, dripping wet and embarrassed, leaped from the table to a lunch lady's lap and then the floor—taking two servings of parsnip ice cream and three water glasses with her.

By now the other five kittens were awake and wanting to get in on the action. Out from under the tables they shot, leaped onto chairs for a better look, then proceeded to the tabletops, which they used the way a frog uses lily pads, jumping from one to the next. Unlike lily pads, however, the tables were laid with rare, historic and breakable glassware.

There was a lot of noise, but—to their credit—the kittens left several things unbroken.

By now the White House staff was mobilizing with mops, brooms and sponges to take back their territory. At the same time, the lunch ladies and gentlemen, used to dealing with food fights worse than this, were assembling to support their allies. In fact, the forces of order probably would have prevailed . . . except that now, from the State Dining Room door, came a truly scary sound, the bugle before the cavalry charge in some classic movie: "*Awh-roohr!*"

Hooligan, worried about his little kitten buddies, had come to the rescue!

Quick as a wink, he did his frenzy thing—lunged forward, thumped his paws, sprang high in the air, then spun so fast he turned blurry.

There are not really English words to describe the effect of a big, clumsy, too-energetic dog on a room containing lots of healthy food, well-dressed people and fancy china, but imagine a furry, dog-smelling blur of noise and destruction on top of six kittens' worth of sharp claws, teeth and caterwauling, and you get the idea.

Lily thought she was watching the circus and kept trying to slip out of her mother's arms to join the fun.

"Maybe if we stay out of the way," Tessa whispered, "no one will remember he's our dog and they're our kittens."

"Right," I said, "and maybe if we close our eyes, we'll disappear."

In the end it was Granny who stopped Hooligan in his tracks, using one of her patented laser glares. Once our dog had been corralled, Mr. Ross, the White House staff and the lunch ladies got the jump on the kittens one by one, then began to sweep up the wreckage.

By eight-thirty, Mom and Aunt Jen had herded the guests into the Entrance Hall so we could say good night. I made sure to apologize to the lunch ladies from Pennsylvania who had sat at our table.

"Oh, don't mention it," said one. "I've been working in school cafeterias for thirty years. A few domestic animals run amok are no problem."

CHAPTER NINE

The second Granny opened the door to say good night, Tessa and I knew we were in trouble.

Tessa spoke first. "It wasn't us that let the Ks out."

Granny crossed her arms over her chest. "It doesn't matter who let them out. They are your pets, and you are responsible. The kittens must go, and the sooner the better."

There is never any point arguing with Granny.

"Yes, ma'am," we said at the same time.

Granny had been standing near the door. Now she walked toward the table that held James Madison's tank. "After what happened this evening," she said, "it seems funny that this is the pet I was worried about. In fact, he's the only one that didn't cause trouble."

Oh, no! In about one second, Granny would look into the tank and see that our cockroach was gone. Was it possible for us to be in more trouble?

"Don't disturb him, Granny!" Tessa said. "He needs his beauty sleep."

Granny looked down into the tank and frowned. "No amount of sleep would make him beautiful."

"Wait," said Tessa, "he's there?"

Granny looked up. "Where else would he be? Oh, no. Don't tell me—"

"Okay, we won't," Tessa said.

I was afraid Granny might ask questions, but instead she checked her watch and announced, "It's almost time for the news with Jan and Larry. They're supposed to have a story on your visit to the zoo today, and I want to see it."

Angry as she was, Granny still kissed us each good night. The door closed. Then Tessa and I waited for a count of five before bouncing up, running across the room and staring down into the tank.

James Madison was there, big as life and relaxing on a magnolia leaf.

Tessa wagged her finger. "You are a bad, bad bug!"

James Madison did not reply.

Had he come back on his own? Had someone brought him back? And where had he been, anyway?

If this really was a mystery, it was getting more mysterious.

CHAPTER TEN

Tessa and I were too tired to stay up talking, so we turned off our lights. I was dreaming of exploding sunflowers when Mom came in.

"Oh, so sorry, muffins," she said. "I didn't realize how late it was, but—to tell you the truth—I miss you."

"That's okay, Mama." Tessa yawned and switched on her lamp. "We miss you, too. Are you mad at us like everybody else is?"

Mom sat down on the edge of Tessa's bed. "I might be if I had the energy. But running the country has tired me out lately."

"Poor Mama. What's the trouble?" Tessa asked.

Mom sighed. "There's more than one, I'm sorry to say. But here's an example. I don't know what to do about those miniaturized drones."

Tessa said, "I happen to know something about drones. They are airplanes without pilots. Does that help?"

"Actually, I already knew that," Mom said.

"So then what's the problem?" Tessa asked.

"Well," Mom said, "Mr. Schott's top secret project is awfully expensive. Also, some people don't like drones."

"You mean because they can spy on people?" I remembered what Nate had said at lunch.

Mom nodded. "Yes, and they can be used as weapons, too. That sounds bad, but drones are good if they help keep Americans safe. Also, Mr. Schott's company employs a lot of workers who need jobs. . . ." She shrugged. "What to do about them is a tough question."

"Mama," said Tessa, "did you know it was going to be so hard to be president?"

Mom nodded. "I had a feeling."

"Then why did you want to do it?"

Mom thought before she answered, "It's a little like solving mysteries, I guess. Even though it's challenging, you girls and Nate do it because it's worthwhile and you're good at it." She shrugged. "Those are basically the same reasons I wanted to be president."

Tessa always has more to say, but that night she didn't have the chance. Mom leaned over and gave her a kiss and a snuggle. Then she came over to my bed, leaned down and gave me a kiss and a snuggle, too.

On her way out the door, Mom said, "One more thing. Please don't tell your friend Courtney my concerns about the drone project. If her father mentions it in his blog, it will only make things worse."

"You don't have to worry about that," said Tessa. "Because Courtney only cares about the bugs."

"The bugs?"

We explained how Courtney thought Mr. Amaro had talked Mom into putting bugs in school lunches.

Mom laughed. "Well, I hope someone set Courtney straight! I have no intention of adding bugs to school lunches."

CHAPTER ELEVEN

Usually the Ks wake us up.

But now the Ks were in not-so-solitary confinement in Hooligan's room—two doors down from ours.

So instead, we were awakened the next morning by people drumming and chanting outside:

"Liberty, equality—set the White House cockroach free!"

Tessa and I rolled over, looked at each other, threw off our covers and ran to the window. The yelling came from a crowd on Pennsylvania Avenue just outside the White House fence. Some of the people carried signs with pictures of butterflies, beetles and grasshoppers. Two women held up a banner between them. It read: BUG LIBERATION FRONT.

Tessa stood next to me. "Cammie, what's 'liberation'?"

"Same as freedom. But I never heard of bug liberation."

"I am all over it," said a voice behind us—Cousin Nate. He and Aunt Jen have an apartment on the White House's third floor. Usually he sleeps as late as he can. The people outside must have waked him, too.

"Don't you know how to knock?" Tessa asked.

"Don't you want to know what the Bug Liberation Front is?" Nate asked.

Unlike some kids I could name (Cammie and Tessa), Nate has his own computer.

"Oh, fine," said Tessa. "What?"

"They're a political group. They believe bugs will inherit the earth, and humans should be nice to them."

Tessa faced the window and waved her arms the way she does. "So what's the problem, people? We are so very nice to James Madison!" She looked around. "Where are my shoes? I am going down there to talk to them."

"No, Tessa, don't!" Nate said. "See, the BLF also believes bugs should not be kept in cages."

"Aha!" Tessa smacked her forehead. "That's the solution to the mystery, then! It was the BLF that let James Madison out yesterday."

"Wait, what? James Madison got out?" Nate said.

"I guess we forgot to tell you," I said. "And I don't think it was the Bug Liberation Front. Because then who put him back? And besides, how would they even know we had a cockroach?"

"True," said Tessa. "And for that matter, how do they even know we have a cockroach now?"

"From Jan and Larry." Granny came in behind Nate. "As I expected, you were on the local news with Jan and Larry last night. They mentioned you'd adopted a cockroach from the zoo. I have to give these bug liberation people credit. They move fast. But now we have more pressing issues to discuss."

"Like how we're not in trouble anymore?" said Tessa hopefully.

"And we don't have to give away the Ks?" I said.

"Actually, you're in more trouble than ever," said Granny. "Wait till you see the news coverage of last night's dinner. But first things first. You have an appointment. Mr. Morgan and Mr. Webb will meet you in the Treaty Room in twenty minutes."

Mr. Morgan and Mr. Webb are security officers who work for the Smithsonian Institution. Sometimes we help them out with detecting. Since the National Zoo is part of the Smithsonian, I was pretty sure I knew what our appointment had to be about—a certain mysterious bug on the run.

As for the news coverage—what was Granny talking about? It couldn't be that the news guys cared about Hooligan and the Ks' minor misbehavior at a formal White House dinner. I mean, could it?

CHAPTER TWELVE

The Treaty Room is across the Center Hall from our bedroom. Sometimes my mom uses it as a second office or for meetings. When Tessa, Nate and I walked in, Mr. Morgan and Mr. Webb were sitting in comfy chairs drinking coffee. As usual, they were wearing rumpled gray suits.

Granny and Mom were also waiting for us in the Treaty Room. If Mom was there, that meant our mystery must be important.

Mom stood up, ruffled Nate's hair and gave me and Tessa each a squeeze.

When she sat back down, she was all business. "Mr. Morgan? Could you go over what you told my national security advisor this morning?"

Tessa was wearing her pink sparkly ball cap, the one she always wears for detecting. I had my pen and notebook, and now I got ready to write.

"Briefly," said Mr. Morgan, "as of twenty-oh-seven

hours yesterday, a government sensing device detected a new radio signal in the White House residence—specifically the East Bedroom."

"Twenty-oh-seven is seven minutes after eight o'clock at night," Nate said.

"We know, Nate," Tessa said.

"And the East Bedroom is our bedroom," I said.

"I know that, too," said Tessa. "And there aren't any signals there, I mean, unless it counts as a signal when the Ks purr. Maybe the device heard the kittens?"

"Impossible," said Mr. Morgan.

"Yeah, Tessa," said Nate. "Because if you remember, at eight-oh-seven last night, your kittens were causing chaos at a White House formal dinner."

"Right!" said Tessa. "Please continue, Mr. Morgan."

Mr. Morgan did. "In fact, we do believe the signal is coming from one of your pets—the newest one, the bug you named James Madison."

Tessa waved her arms. "Oh, fine. Whatever happens, blame the bug."

"I like bugs, actually," said Mr. Morgan. "I had an ant farm as a child."

Tessa's eyes lit up. "Granny? Can we get—"

Granny said, "Don't even think about it."

"Specifically, we believe the signal is coming from an audiovisual transmitter affixed to the bug," said Mr. Morgan.

I looked up from my notebook. "You mean our bug

is shooting video?" I said. "And recording what we say?"

Tessa squealed. "You mean our very own bug is a *spy*?" She smacked her forehead. "And to think all this time we trusted him!"

CHAPTER THIRTEEN

Mr. Morgan did his best to calm Tessa down. "Your bug could hardly have bugged himself," he said. "Therefore, your bug is not the spy. Instead, it appears some other spy is using him for his or her own purposes."

I looked at Tessa. "So whoever stole him yesterday afternoon must've attached a transmitter before they brought him back."

Granny raised her eyebrows. "I don't recall anyone telling me the bug had been stolen."

"That's because you said you didn't want to hear it," said Tessa sweetly. "Remember?"

I explained before Granny could reply. "We noticed the bug was missing at, uh . . . about sixteen-forty-five. He was back when we came in from Mr. Amaro's dinner at, uh . . . twenty thirty hundred hours. That's four-forty-five till eight-thirty in regular-people time, not quite four hours."

Mr. Morgan nodded. "And presumably he had been

returned by twenty-oh-seven when the device picked up the signal from your bedroom."

"But wait a second," Tessa said. "We've seen our bug since he came back. There's no camera attached to him. He just looks regular."

Mr. Morgan nodded. "With miniaturization technology, the transmitter could be very tiny. It may also have been camouflaged—painted to match the cockroach."

Mom cleared her throat and looked at her watch. "If you'll excuse me, I have a meeting with Mr. Schott and the joint chiefs five minutes ago. What is it you want the children to do, gentlemen?"

Mr. Morgan said, "Find out who bugged the bug."

Mr. Webb nodded.

Mom stood up. "All right, fine. Provided, of course"— she looked at Granny—"you think it's safe?"

"I think we can keep it safe, yes," said Granny.

Mom nodded. "Good luck, muffins. You, too, Nate. I'll talk to you tonight."

Mr. Morgan and Mr. Webb stood up. Mom shook hands with each of them. When she was gone, Mr. Webb took a crumpled piece of paper from his vest pocket and handed it to Mr. Morgan, who looked it over.

"This is our plan of action," Mr. Morgan said. "The first step is to disable the transmitter. However, I must warn you. Our technician cannot ensure your pet's structural integrity."

Tessa looked at Nate. "Translation?"

"He means when they unhook the transmitter,

they might squash James Madison by accident," Nate explained.

Tessa looked horrified. "That is not okay! And anyway, who cares what goes on in Cammie's and my room? We hardly have any secrets . . . I mean, unless you count the snack stash in Cammie's underwear drawer."

Granny said, "What snack stash?" at the same time that I said, "How did you know about that?" and Nate said, "Anything good?"

Mr. Morgan wasn't interested in my snacks. "I think you underestimate the risks," he said. "All sorts of people could be interested in something you girls say, or something your parents or grandmother says to you—a foreign power, a reporter, even the political opposition. You may not even realize what you know and what you talk about."

"He has a point, Tessa." I remembered how Mom had told us her worries over Mr. Schott's drone last night.

Tessa said, "But that doesn't mean you can just go squishing my pet!"

In our family, I am quiet, Tessa is loud, and Nate is smart. Now I thought of something that might be a good idea, but—not being either smart or loud—I felt shy about saying it.

"Uh . . . ," I mumbled.

"Go ahead, Cameron," said Granny.

"Well," I finally said, "what if we leave the transmitter alone?"

Nate twirled his finger next to his head—*crazy*—

and pointed at me. The grown-ups shook their heads. Even Tessa looked doubtful.

Oh, fine. What else had I expected?

Still, I tried to explain: If we left the transmitter alone, the spy—whoever it was—wouldn't know we were investigating. On the other hand, if we took the transmitter off, the spy would see us doing it. And then he (or she?) would do his best to hide his tracks.

Mr. Morgan nodded thoughtfully. "Good point," he said.

"Thank you," I said.

There was more discussion. But Granny's vote was the one that counted. When she said we should try my plan, I—for once—felt smart.

"All right then, it's decided," said Mr. Morgan. "But please remember this. You kids must be very careful what you say in front of the bug. Because we have no idea who it is that's listening, a single slipup could endanger not only you and your family but the entire United States of America."

CHAPTER FOURTEEN

Before he and Mr. Webb left, Mr. Morgan asked us to do one more thing—take a look at our cockroach and see if we could spot the transmitter.

"What does a transmitter even look like?" Tessa asked.

Mr. Morgan said, "It will be the part of the bug that doesn't look like a bug."

I scratched my head. Was that supposed to be helpful?

Granny told us to meet her and Nate for breakfast in the Family Kitchen in ten minutes. I should bring my notebook so we could get right to work detecting.

But first Tessa and I went to wash up and take a good look at our cockroach.

The two of us had been in our room about five seconds when I realized that life with a bugged bug was not going to be easy.

Challenge No. 1: How do you look for a transmitter without looking like you're looking for a transmitter? Finally, I said, "Oh, Tessa. I am so worried about our cockroach, James Madison!"

I tried very hard to sound exactly normal, but Tessa squinted like I was acting weird.

"I mean"—I nodded at the tank—"didn't James Madison appear a teeny bit sick this morning? He might have a case of the sniffles. We had better look at him very closely to make sure he is healthy."

Tessa said, "I don't think cockroaches get sniffles."

Now I was exasperated. "Tessa, would you for gosh sake get with the program?"

"What are you talking—Oh!" Tessa finally caught on and tried to sound exactly normal, too. "Yes, Cameron. You are so correct. We had better look at James Madison closely. Also, you should get a tissue in case we have to wipe his nose."

I got a tissue. Then the two of us knelt by the tank and stared. James Madison stared back. I thought of how some spying stranger was probably staring at us on a video screen, his version of Bug TV.

I couldn't help it. I crossed my eyes and stuck out my tongue.

Then I got serious. Was there anything different about our cockroach today? Maybe the government sensing device was wrong. Maybe there had never been a new signal.

But wait! Now that I looked harder, I did see

something: James Madison used to have two horns on his head, and now there was a third one—right between the others. Could it be a camera lens? Also, there was a narrow black band like a belt around his middle. Maybe attached to the band was a microphone? Maybe the microphone was painted cockroach orange?

I tried to imagine how the bad guy had attached the tiny equipment to Tessa's and my bug. Tiny belt buckles? Tiny Velcro? Tiny laces?

I knew Tessa had seen the same things I saw. I knew she was dying to point them out. But instead she said, "I have looked and looked but do not see a trace of cockroach snot, Cameron. Do you?"

"Not a trace," I said. "He looks exactly as healthy as he did yesterday before he went on the run."

"Phew!" Tessa wiped imaginary sweat from her forehead. "I am so relieved! Now, dear sister, shall we go and have a lovely breakfast with our grandmother and cousin?"

On our way to breakfast, we took a quick detour to the window above the North Portico. Only a few members of the Bug Liberation Front remained out front. I wondered where the other ones had gone.

CHAPTER FIFTEEN

Depending on how you count, there are at least three kitchens in the White House. Our family's is next to the second-floor dining room, just off the West Sitting Hall. When we walked in, Nate was pouring milk, Hooligan was dreaming under the table, Mr. Bryant was reading the newspaper, and Humdinger, Granny's canary, was doing a canary dance-and-song—*twee-twee-twee*—in his cage by the window.

Here's the best part: Granny was standing at the griddle, spatula in hand, cooking banana pancakes!

We said good morning to Mr. Bryant. For the past couple of months, he and Granny have been special friends, so I could be pretty sure she had told him already about our bugged bug.

Mr. Bryant said good morning back, then held up the front page of the *Washington Post* for us to see. On it was a huge picture of Fluffy sailing across the State Dining Room toward the sunflower arrangement at the dinner last night. The headline said: MEOW! WHITE HOUSE PETS OUT OF CONTROL?

"Uh-oh," said Tessa and I at the same time.

"Hmph," said Granny. "The sooner those kittens of yours are gone, the happier I'll be. Now, who wants pancakes?"

I got milk and maple syrup from the refrigerator. Tessa got silverware from the drawer. As she and I set the table, we took turns telling everyone about James Madison's new horn and new stripe.

Granny served the pancakes and sat down. "I'll pass that information to Mr. Morgan and Mr. Webb," she said. "Now then, Cameron. While we eat, what if you share your notes with us? That way everyone can help."

Between bites, I read my notes out loud. When you're detecting, the next step after you take notes is to identify anything in them that seems strange, important, or both.

Nate spoke first. "I have a question. Did you guys know when you went to the zoo that you were going to adopt a cockroach?"

"Nope," said Tessa. "It was just a good idea I had when the zookeeper told me he had an extra."

"In that case," said Nate, "whoever bugged James Madison didn't have time to plan."

"Write that down, Cammie," Tessa said.

"I will," I said.

"And he couldn't have come from the zoo already bugged," Granny added. "It must have happened here at the White House."

"Something else," said Nate. "Our spy has to be an expert on technology, someone who knows about miniaturized microphones and cameras, not to mention how to attach them to cockroaches."

"Write that—"

"I am, Tessa!"

Mr. Bryant took a sip of coffee, set his mug on the table and touched his napkin to his lips. "Perhaps this seems obvious," he said. "However, I am struck by the fact that our culprit had access to the White House second floor. As you well know, the building is secure. Only select staff, family and guests are allowed upstairs."

Ick! It was creepy to think a spy had been in our room! And even more creepy to think the spy might be someone we knew.

"What are the times again, Cammie?" Tessa wanted to know.

I turned back a couple of pages. "Whoever borrowed James Madison had to have done it while we were outside. So that means between about two o'clock and four-forty-five yesterday."

Tessa nodded. "Then the person was in our room again at eight-oh-seven, because that's when the government device first detected the signal coming from there."

Granny said, "Mr. Amaro's dinner was still in progress at that time. So everyone at the dinner has an alibi."

"That makes me think of something," said Nate. "Mr. Amaro left the dinner early. Remember? The lunch ladies from Pennsylvania were awfully disappointed when he didn't take questions."

"It could be that someone else left the dinner early as well," said Mr. Bryant. "But not everyone has access to the second floor, as Mr. Amaro does."

Tessa said, "Plus, he likes bugs. Woo-hoo! A for-real suspect! I think we're going to have to ask that gentleman just a few simple questions."

In case you can't tell, my sister's favorite part of detecting is asking suspects questions.

"But why would a chef want to spy on the White House?" I asked. "Mr. Amaro doesn't have a motive."

"Well, if you're looking for a motive," Tessa said, "I know who has one: Mr. Lozana! His blog would be a lot more interesting if he had a secret spy in the White House."

"It's true that Mr. Lozana knew about the cockroach. He was also upstairs yesterday afternoon," Granny said.

"But Courtney has been my best friend forever!" I said. "And Mr. Lozana wasn't ever in the White House last night."

"Not as far as we know," said Nate.

Tessa shrugged. "Write down Mr. Lozana as a maybe suspect, Cammie. It can't hurt to ask Courtney some questions, right?"

Reluctantly, I wrote Mr. Lozana's name.

Meanwhile, our plates began to rattle. Hooligan, awake and scrabbling to his feet, had caused a table quake! It took a few seconds for him to sort out his paws and tail; then he seated himself by my chair and looked up with heartbreak in his eyes. He had just realized the banana pancakes were gone.

"Come on, old man." Mr. Bryant scratched behind Hooligan's ears. "Let's the two of us go for a little walk. Would anyone like to join us?"

Nate said, "I have to practice piano."

My cousin is some kind of piano genius, so—except when he's studying a kind of arithmetic I can't even pronounce—he usually has to practice piano.

"Why don't you girls go put on your sneakers and head out, too?" Granny said. "I understand Mr. Amaro is supposed to be in the Kitchen Garden this morning. Something about tomatoes. If you want to ask him some questions, you can probably catch up with him there."

Tessa and I got up to go. Then I remembered something. "Granny—James Madison needs breakfast, too. Have you got anything he might like?"

CHAPTER SIXTEEN

Back in our room, Mrs. Hedges was changing the sheets on our beds.

"More laundry. More work for me. And all those houseguests, too," she muttered.

Tessa and I read each other's thoughts. James Madison's microphone was hearing Mrs. Hedges's complaints. What if the spy who was watching Bug TV told the world our family was mean to people who work in the White House? This could make our mom look bad!

Tessa said, "Mrs. Hedges, are you working too hard?"

Mrs. Hedges hadn't heard us come in. Now she jumped. "Don't sneak up on me!"

I said, "Maybe you'd like to sit down and take a break."

"I could get you a cup of tea," Tessa said. "Or how about lemonade?"

Mrs. Hedges frowned. "Why are you being so nice all of a sudden?"

"We're always nice!" I said.

Mrs. Hedges put her hands over her ears. "Well, you don't need to shout about it." Then she softened up. "I said good morning to James Madison when I came in. I'm not sure, but I think he waved an antenna back."

"Would you like to feed him?" I held up the breakfast Granny had given me.

"He likes banana peels?" Mrs. Hedges said.

"Cockroaches have many fine qualities," I said. "And one is that they're not picky eaters."

Mrs. Hedges opened the lid of James Madison's tank and laid the peel on the dirt. Then we put the lid back on and hooked it closed. Soon James Madison ambled over and stood on top of his breakfast.

"I think he's interested," Tessa said.

"But not enthusiastic," said Mrs. Hedges.

"Maybe we should try stale taco chips," I said. "The zookeeper called them a cockroach favorite."

"Only not the spicy ones," Tessa reminded me. "Those give him a tummyache."

We watched James Madison consider his breakfast for a few moments more. Then Tessa and I put on our sneakers and Mrs. Hedges finished with the sheets.

"Feeding the cockroach was probably the highlight of my day," she said, picking up the laundry basket. "Now, if you'll excuse me, I have an endless number of beds to change."

As soon as she was gone, Tessa turned to me. "Got your notebook, Cammie?"

"Uh, not yet," I said. "There's something I have to tell you."

"Oka-a-ay . . . ," said Tessa. "What?"

Now what? The something was something I couldn't say in front of James Madison, but Tessa didn't know that. She frowned, tapped her foot and checked her Barbie watch.

Then I had an idea. "Tessa, remember how the zookeeper told us that in Madagascar cockroaches always live near waterfalls?"

"Nope," Tessa said unhelpfully.

"Well, dear sister, that is exactly what the zookeeper told us. So now, how about if we put James Madison's tank in the bathroom where he can listen to the sound of running water and feel at home?"

I could see from Tessa's face that she wanted to say I was crazy, but then, all of a sudden, she caught on. "Oh! Why, Cameron," she said in her most normal possible voice, "what an excellent idea!"

Together, we picked up the tank, carried it to the bathroom, turned the water on, walked out and closed the door.

"That was good thinking," Tessa said. "Only we can't do it for very long, because it wastes water."

"I know, but this is an emergency. From now on, we need to keep James Madison with us all the time."

Tessa made a face. "All the time?"

"Look what just happened with Mrs. Hedges," I said. "She talks to herself when she's cleaning. What if she gives away a secret and endangers the United

States of America? Or what about this? The spy could sneak in again and let James Madison loose to snoop other places—like in one of Mom's meetings."

Tessa looked alarmed. "Uh-oh. But how do we carry him with us?"

"In that little plastic box the zoo gave us, remember? It's in my desk drawer."

The clear plastic box was a disk about half an inch high and three inches in diameter. After we returned James Madison's tank to its table, Tessa took him out and packed him inside with a leaf and a strip of banana peel. It was a tight squeeze, but the keeper had said cockroaches in the wild live mostly in holes, so to a cockroach, squished just feels cozy.

Tessa snapped the box shut and said, "There you are, James Madison. Your own personal mobile home."

"And now we're going on a field trip," I said. "You're really going to like the weather outside. It's hot, just like your native Madagascar."

CHAPTER SEVENTEEN

I changed into cargo shorts so I'd have a pocket for James Madison's mobile home, then—along with Tessa—went downstairs to meet Mr. Bryant and Hooligan under the awning outside the Diplomatic Reception Room. It's on the ground floor and our most usual way in and out of the White House.

"What's Mr. Amaro doing out here again?" Tessa asked Mr. Bryant as we walked.

"Picking tomatoes," Mr. Bryant said. "The idea is to encourage people to grow vegetables as well as eat them. The ladies and gentlemen of the Fourth Estate are going to snap some pictures of him and his harvest."

"Fourth Estate means news guys," I explained before Tessa could ask.

"The news guys are gonna be there?" said Tessa. "That gives me an idea."

"What?" I asked.

"Don't worry, Cammie," my sister said. "We could hardly be in any more trouble, right?"

The South Lawn is as big as fourteen football fields, and the Kitchen Garden is at the far end. It was a long walk in air that felt like chicken soup. I was sweaty by the time we saw the garden and the news guys clustered around it. Soon after that, we saw something else—Bug Liberation Front protesters outside the fence on Executive Drive.

So that was where the rest of them had gone!

"Hey, Fireball and Fussbudget—yo!" Charlotte caught up to us. "What happened to Fingers?"

Everyone in our family has a Secret Service code name. Fireball is Tessa, and Fussbudget's me. Nate is Fingers because, like I said—piano genius.

"Practicing piano," said Tessa.

"Of course he is," said Charlotte.

Tessa, Nate and I are not allowed to be outside without Secret Service protection, and there are always agents posted on the lawn. Some of them wear suits, but some of them wear casual clothes so you'd think they're just regular people hanging out.

As we approached the garden, Mr. Bryant made a hard left to avoid the news guys. The White House pets did not need more publicity. We could meet up later. The Kitchen Garden is about the same size as a big bedroom, and its pattern of rows and squares reminds me of a quilt. Besides tomatoes, there are kale, peas, corn, eggplants, okra, Brussels sprouts and herbs. There are raspberry bushes, too, and off to the side, a couple of beehives.

Ms. Major was waiting for us, along with a White House photographer and the White House head gardener.

"What are the Bug Liberation Front protesters doing down here?" I asked Ms. Major.

"They must've got wind of Chef Amaro's plan for a photo op, and now they're hoping the press will pay attention to them, too," Ms. Major said.

"Look, here he comes!" Tessa pointed at an orange mini-tractor speeding toward us with Mr. Amaro driving. His sequined turquoise bandanna and wraparound glasses made him easy to recognize. Some of the protesters recognized him, too. One of them had a guitar and strummed it, waving and hooting at the same time.

Mr. Amaro waved and hooted back.

Then the protesters started another chant:

"Fish gotta swim, birds gotta fly,
Bugs gotta roam or else they die."

Instead of watching where he was going, Mr. Amaro was reading the signs—and soon the tractor was heading straight for us!

Everybody ran for their lives.

"Look out!" Charlotte yelled.

Mr. Amaro turned his head, saw the crash-about-to-happen and yanked the wheel just in time. The tractor jerked to a halt at the very edge of the garden, its tires spinning up a messy spray of grass and dirt.

Phew! My heart was pounding. But Mr. Amaro didn't seem to notice he'd almost taken out half a dozen news guys and a row of arugula. He just hopped off the tractor and grinned his famous grin. "Hey, everybody. Awesome to be here!"

CHAPTER EIGHTEEN

As you'd expect from a pro-vegetable TV star, Mr. Amaro had no trouble being photographed and picking tomatoes at the same time. He even showed Tessa and me how. What you do is kneel in the dirt, hunt until you find a red one, grab gently and twist hard till it separates from the stem. Tomato stems, in case you don't know, are smelly and covered with sticky, silvery hairs.

Anyway, after that, if the tomato is round enough and pretty enough, you hold it beside your smiling face, look up at the photographer and try not to blink while the sweat drips in your eyes.

"Lovely, Tessa!" said the photographer. "Uh, Cameron? Wipe the dirt smudge off your nose and we'll try it again."

After the photos were done, I reached for the notebook in my pocket and touched something round and smooth—James Madison's mobile home.

That's when—duh—I realized something you probably figured out a mile ago.

Tessa and I had a big problem!

How were we supposed to interview a suspect about a bugged bug when the bugged bug could hear every one of our questions?

"Tessa, wait!" I pulled James Madison out of my pocket and showed her.

"Uh-oh," said Tessa.

Meanwhile, Ms. Major, the photographer and the news guys also caught sight of James Madison, and there was a general chorus of *"Ewwwww!"*

The protesters must've known *"Ewwwww"* referred to the cockroach because they started chanting again:

"Two, four, six, eight,
Who ya gonna liberate?
Cockroach! Cockroach! Yeah!"

The slogan gave me an idea. "James Madison," I said, "how would you like to romp in the dirt and sunshine for a few minutes? And meanwhile maybe Charlotte could bug-sit?"

Charlotte blinked. "I'm pretty sure bug-sitting is not part of my job description."

Tessa flashed one of her world-famous smiles. "Pretty please?"

Charlotte sniffed. "Oh, all right. As long as I don't have to touch him."

I twisted the lid off James Madison's box and dumped him—gently—out. Preceded by his curious antennae, he ambled off toward the basil, zucchini and bush beans.

"Now, Mr. Amaro," said Tessa. "If you'll step this way? I have just a few questions."

CHAPTER NINETEEN

Mr. Amaro, Tessa and I walked to the other side of the Kitchen Garden, where James Madison couldn't hear us. Tessa crossed her arms over her chest, getting ready to ask questions. But before she did, I wanted to say something: "We're really sorry about our pets last night at the dinner, Mr. Amaro. They don't mean to be bad. They just have too much energy."

Mr. Amaro laughed. "Are you kidding? They were awesome! I never got so much publicity for a gig in all my years as a celebrity chef."

"So you're not mad?" Tessa said.

"Not me, chickadee," said Mr. Amaro.

"In that case," said Tessa, "where did you go last night when you had to leave the dinner early? Were you upstairs in our room putting James Madison back in his tank?"

My sister does not fool around when she interviews a suspect.

Mr. Amaro looked puzzled. "Say what?"

I tried to help him out. "You can skip the second part if you want."

"Awesome," said Mr. Amaro. "As for where I went when I left the dinner—that was to the restroom. It was, uh . . . kind of an emergency."

"Which restroom?" Tessa asked.

Mr. Amaro raised his eyebrows. "You sure you want the details?"

My little sister doesn't like to talk about burps, let alone restrooms. She shook her head. "That's okay. Forget I asked. And I guess you don't have proof?"

"Ick!" said Mr. Amaro.

"How about a new line of questioning?" I suggested.

"Good idea," said Tessa. "Mr. Amaro, where were you yesterday after lunch?"

"Why, I was in and out of the kitchen all afternoon, helping to make dinner. There's a pile o' witnesses if you need 'em. But what's the deal, huh? Are the famous White House sleuths investigating a case? Hey"—he grinned—"and am I a suspect? How cool is that? Who is it you think I murdered?"

"We mostly investigate stolen things," I said.

"And I only have one more question," Tessa said. "What do you know about teeny tiny transmitters?"

Mr. Amaro shrugged. "Not much anymore. I was a radio guy in the army, but that was a long time ago, and the technology has changed." He pulled out his phone to check the time. "Will that do ya? I've got a meeting with the ambassador from a certain nearby nation."

"No kidding?" said Tessa. "His niece is our friend, Toni. We gave them their dog!"

"Awesome!" said Mr. Amaro. "The deal is their president wants a personal chef. Could be a good gig." He shrugged. "I like to travel."

Walking back around the Kitchen Garden, I was thinking Mr. Amaro was still a suspect. He hadn't been in the kitchen every minute of the afternoon. He could've been lying about the restroom. And maybe he knew more about radios than he would admit.

As for his motive, could it be something to do with a certain nearby nation? There had been political trouble there lately. And Mr. Morgan had said whoever bugged the bug might be from a foreign power.

Mr. Amaro was about to hop up on the mini-tractor when all of a sudden he shrieked and staggered back.

"What's the matter?" I asked.

Breathing fast, Mr. Amaro pointed at the tractor seat: "Sp-sp-sp-spider!"

Tessa said, "No lie?" and leaned in to get a better look. "Hey, guy!" she said, then scooped the tiny spider up in her palm. "Awww, he's just little. Look."

Mr. Amaro shuddered and waved her away. "I can't stand creepy crawlies."

"Wait a sec," I said. "Didn't you say eating bugs is a good idea?"

"Only dead bugs," he clarified. "And I know I'm a wimp, but I had a bad experience with a beetle in pre-school. Did you, uh . . . take care of that spider, Tessa?"

Tessa held up her empty hands. "I put him in the parsley."

Mr. Amaro breathed a sigh of relief and climbed aboard the tractor. "Awesome. Good luck finding your thief, ladies!"

Tessa said, "Thanks."

I said, "Drive carefully."

Mr. Amaro turned the key, waved to the crowd by the fence, spun the steering wheel and sped off.

"I need to talk to the news guys for a sec," said Tessa. "And don't ask why, 'cause you don't want to know."

"You're right. I don't," I said, and looked around till I found Charlotte.

"Thanks for watching James Madison," I told her.

"You're welcome," said Charlotte. Then she looked down at the dirt in front of her, frowned and looked back up at me. "Oops."

CHAPTER TWENTY

Charlotte felt really terrible about losing James Madison. "I didn't know he could move that fast! They don't cover foreign cockroaches at the Secret Service academy."

By now, Tessa had come back from her secret mission to the news guys. She waved her arms. "Well, they should!" Then she called: "James Madison! He-e-ere, James Madison!"

I thought of something and whispered in Tessa's ear.

My sister squealed. "How could you even whisper such a thing? James Madison is our pet! Of course it would be bad if he disappeared forever!"

Aargh—was Tessa ever going to learn to be careful about what she said? Just because we couldn't see the cockroach didn't mean he couldn't hear us!

"I think we need reinforcements," said Charlotte; then she spoke into her radio. "Charlotte to base— we've got a kind of a situation here. Is the secret weapon available? Over." There was a pause, and then she cocked her head. "Roger that. We'll expect him in five."

While the three of us waited, we looked for the missing bug, but all we got for our trouble was dirty hands and knees. Finally, there was a fuss behind us. Then someone yelled: "Incoming!"

We knew what that meant. Our secret weapon was about to make his entrance. As usual, it was grand. Tail and ears flying, he galloped a fast lap around the garden, then made a graceful flying leap right at me and my sister.

He only wanted to say "Glad to see you!"

He wasn't trying to knock anybody over.

Still, he knocked somebody over.

"Ouch, puppy," said Tessa from where she lay on the grass.

Hooligan, sometimes known as our secret weapon, circled back and licked her face to apologize.

"Never mind." Tessa sat up and wiped off the dog slobber. "Do we have anything that smells like cockroach, Cammie?"

I knelt, twisted the lid off James Madison's empty mobile home and stuck it in front of Hooligan's nose. "This is what we're looking for," I said.

Hooligan sniffed the plastic and scarfed down the leftover banana peel. "Can you do it, puppy?" I asked.

"Of course he can!" said Tessa. "Hooligan, go find!"

You may have noticed that our secret weapon has a mind of his own.

What we expected him to do was bury his nose in the dirt and sniff. What he actually did was raise his head, perk up his ears and listen.

Did he hear the hiss of a missing cockroach? He definitely heard something. And whatever it was caused him to plow into the green tangle of garden, trampling everything in his path.

"My oregano!" The White House head gardener closed his eyes. "I can't watch."

Lucky for the oregano, the doggy destruction lasted only a few moments; then Hooligan lowered his head and snatched something in his fearsome jaws.

I couldn't see what it was, but I could hear: "*Sssss!*"

CHAPTER TWENTY-ONE

Even if cockroaches like cozy spaces, the inside of a dog's mouth is not that comfortable. I know because of the desperate way James Madison wiggled his legs and antennae.

"Go-o-o-od puppy," Tessa cooed at Hooligan. "Don't crunch. Just give him over."

Hooligan considered obeying but then had a better idea. He pulled back, thumped his paws, threw his head from side to side and growled: Cockroach tug-o'-war! Doggy fun at its finest!

Tessa was not amused. She put her hands on her hips and did her best impression of Granny. "Drop it."

Hooligan dropped it.

Meanwhile, I was wondering how the last few minutes had looked to the spy watching and listening to Bug TV. First there had been darkness in my pocket, then a sunny garden with an herb jungle and mountain-sized zucchini.

After that came the slobbery pink inside of Hooligan's

mouth with its border of treacherous, pointy teeth, and the lurching side-to-side fun-house-in-space while Hooligan swung his head.

Was the spy watching live right now? Or would he watch the footage recorded later? Either way, it was going to make him dizzy.

At last, Tessa got hold of James Madison, who was sticky with dog slobber and streaked with dirt. She pulled a tissue from her pocket and dabbed James Madison's . . . uh . . . face. It was hard to tell if this made him any cleaner.

Trying to sound exactly normal, I said, "Tessa, our cousin Nathan should be finished with practicing piano by now. Let us go back up to the house and have a pleasant chat with him, shall we?"

"Yeah, we gotta work on the case some more," Tessa said. "Did you believe Mr. Amaro when he said he had to leave the dinner—Hey! That hurt! Why did you kick me?"

I raised my eyebrows and nodded at James Madison. "Remember?"

"Right!" my sister said. "And you know what, Cammie? I think I'm just going to be quiet while we walk back to the White House."

CHAPTER TWENTY-TWO

There are three elevators in the White House.

The fanciest one is the Family Elevator. On the ground floor, it opens across the Center Hall from the Diplomatic Reception Room, also known as the Dip Room. How fancy is the Family Elevator?

So fancy it has wood paneling. So fancy there has to be an operator to make it work. So fancy that the operator always wears a tuxedo. So fancy that a First Lady a long time ago tried to make it a rule that the staff wasn't even allowed to use it, only the president's family.

Mr. Bryant used to have the elevator job before he got a new job watching Hooligan. Now the elevator operator is Mr. Jackson. He's nice, and he usually knows all about anything going on in the White House.

Tessa must have been thinking about Mr. Jackson while she walked silently across the South Lawn from the Kitchen Garden. In the Dip Room, she tugged my arm.

"What about if you take the stairs, dear sister?" she asked—sounding exactly normal. "While I, instead, ascend in the elevator?"

I almost argued. I had walked just as far as she had, hadn't I? And if anything, I was sweatier. But then she winked about twelve times and pointed at the pocket where James Madison was—and I caught on. If she took the elevator, she could ask Mr. Jackson questions without James Madison hearing.

I winked back and gave her a thumbs-up.

Back in our bedroom, I put James Madison away in his tank, then went to wash my hands. Taped to the bathroom mirror was a note from Granny. It said: *Don't forget to give away the kittens.*

When I came out, Tessa was there, and I handed her the note.

"But I don't want to!" she wailed.

"I know, Tessa. I don't, either. But we can't win this fight because we can't have Granny mad at us forever. If you get the art stuff, we can make flyers that say 'Kittens free to good home.' Nate will help us. Plenty of people work in the White House. If we post them, somebody nice will take the Ks."

Since we wanted to talk about the case while we worked, we had to get James Madison out of the way. Luckily, I had an idea. Our secret weapon is not only good at finding things, he has a built-in alarm system, too.

So I went to find Mr. Bryant and ask if Hooligan was available.

Ten minutes later, Hooligan was guarding James Madison in our room, and Tessa, Nate and I were seated at a round table in the West Sitting Hall. We had laid newspaper out on the table so we didn't make a mess. In front of each of us was a stack of paper. In the middle of the table was a pile of markers. We had glue and glitter just in case we got inspired.

"I am not a very good artist," Nate said after we explained about the kitten flyers.

"Wait—you mean there's something you're not good at?" I said.

Nate said, "Very funny."

My family has lived in Washington since my mom was elected senator from California seven years ago. Nate and Aunt Jen moved here from San Diego in January when Mom got to be president and our family came to live in the White House. At first, my cousin always acted *so* superior, but after being around nice, normal kids like Tessa and me, he's improved a lot.

"If you don't want to draw, you can read the notes from my interview with Mr. Amaro," I told Nate.

Tessa said, "We can skip that part. Mr. Amaro didn't bug the bug."

Nate and I looked at each other. Then we looked at Tessa. Trying to act casual, she picked up a black marker and drew two kitten ears.

"Oh, so now who's acting 'so superior'?" I asked.

Tessa giggled. "I know, right? I figured it out all by myself. Mr. Amaro was scared of the eensy teensy spider. No way could he have picked up a giant hissing cockroach!"

"What spider?" Nate asked.

I explained.

Nate nodded. "Well, in that case—duh! Of course Tessa's right. I don't see why you didn't figure that out, too, Cammie."

I ignored this comment. "I guess for now we can cross Mr. Amaro off our list. Tessa, what did Mr. Jackson say about who rode his elevator last night?"

Tessa picked up a red marker. "Only Mr. Schott."

Nate said, "Of course! We should've thought of him sooner. He for sure has the technical knowledge. And he's a guest, so he can go on the second floor without anybody questioning him."

"He also wanted to take pictures of James Madison yesterday afternoon," Tessa said. "But what's his motive?"

"Something to do with that drone project he's working on?" I said, and I was going to go on, but Nate shushed me. Mrs. Verity and Lily were coming down the hall. The second Lily spotted Tessa, she ran for her full-speed.

"What you doing?" Lily wanted to know.

"Making pictures," Tessa said.

"Can I hep?" Lily asked. "Pee-eeze?"

"Sure," Tessa said.

Lily took her mom's hand. "We go get paint."

"Paint? We don't have any paint," Mrs. Verity said.

"Yeah, we do, Mommy. I show you." Lily took her mom's hand and tugged her back down the hall.

Mrs. Verity looked over her shoulder at us and smiled. "Be right back."

"So what's the plan? What do we do next?" Nate asked.

"Interview Mr. Schott," I said.

"What about Mr. Lozana?" said Tessa.

I shook my head. "Not this again. I know you think he has a motive, Tessa. But Courtney's my best friend! And anyway, he wasn't in the White House last night."

"Actually, he was." Tessa pointed at the newspaper on the table. It was the one with the photo of Fluffy on the front page, and now I noticed something for the first time—the lunch ladies and other people behind Fluffy. One of them was Mr. Lozana.

"What's he doing there?" Nate asked. "He wasn't invited to the dinner."

"I'm sure there's a perfectly good explanation," I said.

"Unh-hunh," said Tessa.

"And besides," I said, "Mr. Schott is staying here in the White House. He's easier to interview."

Tessa frowned. "But I don't like him."

"Tessa," I said, "since when did we ever solve a mystery interviewing only people we like?"

Tessa by now was lettering her second flyer. "You're right. So next let's interview Courtney."

"Thanks a lot!" I said, ready to defend my friend, but Lily and her mom were coming back.

"It turned out my daughter meant nail polish when she said paint." Mrs. Verity smiled. "I told her it doesn't work well on paper, and besides, the bottle's almost empty."

Lily climbed onto Tessa's lap. Tessa said, "Do you want to do the stickers?"

"Yes, peeze," said Lily.

"Do you kids mind if I leave her with you for a few minutes?" Mrs. Verity asked. "I need to track down my husband."

"Sure, we'll watch her," Tessa said.

"Thanks a billion," said Mrs. Verity. "Be good, Lily."

When Mrs. Verity was gone, Nate frowned. "Now we can't talk about you know what."

"Yeah, we can," said Tessa. "Little kids don't understand that much. Do you, Lily?"

Lily was unsticking a skeleton from a sheet of leftover Halloween stickers. "Nope," she said.

"In that case, what about physical evidence?" Nate asked. "You know—clues like fingerprints on the cockroach tank."

"They'd be all mixed up and smudged," I said. "We didn't know to be careful till it was too late."

I had finished three flyers by now. I was getting more paper when a terrible and familiar noise—"*Awhroohr!*"—made all of us jump and look at each other.

Someone had breached cockroach security. The Hooligan alarm was sounding!

CHAPTER TWENTY-THREE

I covered the distance from the West Sitting Hall to our bedroom in record time. When I got there, the door was open and the dog was howling.

But whoever had tripped the alarm was gone.

"Good puppy—you can turn it off now!" I ran past Hooligan to check the tank. The lid was still on top, but was James Madison inside?

I had to stare for a moment, but then a couple of twigs rustled and finally two curious black antennae appeared.

By this time, Nate, Tessa and Lily were standing beside me. "Do you think he's okay?" Tessa asked.

I caught my breath before answering. "Why, of course, dear sister," I said, sounding exactly normal. "Our pet is perfectly fine."

"But what about the spy—" Tessa started to ask, but then she interrupted herself. "Never mind. Uh, Cameron? Our pet has had such a stressful day. Maybe he would feel better if he could listen to that calming waterfall sound from his childhood?"

"Good idea," I said, and together we carried the tank into the bathroom and turned on the water.

"Nate says you guys kwazy," Lily said when we came out again.

"Because they are," said Nate.

"But now we can talk without the bug listening," I said. "Someone came in, set off the doggy alarm and ran away. Was it the spy?"

"Or maybe just Mrs. Hedges," said Nate.

"Why would Hooligan howl at Mrs. Hedges?" Tessa asked. "And even if he did, she wouldn't run away. She's not afraid of Hooligan."

I looked down at our dog, who was sitting beside me looking up hopefully, expecting his doggy reward. Unfortunately, I was fresh out. "Sorry, puppy," I said.

"Give him a pretzel," said Tessa.

"Who says I've got a pretzel?" I asked.

"Pretzuh?" said Lily.

"You have them in your secret snack stash," said Nate.

Hooligan woofed hopefully.

"Oh, fine." I went to my dresser and opened my underwear drawer.

"You know, Cammie, we've been working hard, too," said Tessa.

Lily nodded. "Vewy hawd."

I passed around my last bag of pretzels. We were

crunching when we heard Mrs. Verity's voice from the Center Hall. "Lily?"

"We're in here!" Tessa answered.

Mrs. Verity appeared in our doorway. She was dressed all glamorous in a clingy gold gown. Her blond hair was pinned up. She had on a lot of eye shadow.

"Wow, you look like a Barbie!" said Tessa.

"Thanks . . . I think," said Mrs. Verity.

"Did you find Mr. Verity?" Tessa asked.

"Max is working on it for me," Mrs. Verity said. Then she looked down at Lily. "Did you do anything fun with the big kids, sweet pea?"

"Eat pretzuhs and talk 'bout spies," Lily said.

Mrs. Verity winked at us. "Spies and pretzels? Well, isn't that nice? Come along now. Kids, I can't thank you enough."

When they were gone, Tessa, Nate and I looked at each other. Spies? Uh-oh. Maybe talking in front of a little kid hadn't been such a good idea.

CHAPTER TWENTY-FOUR

There was still an hour before dinner. If we hurried, we could squeeze in one more round of detecting. I told Nate and Tessa my plan.

"Wait—I have to take the bug?" Nate said.

"You don't even have to touch him," I said.

We retrieved James Madison from the bathroom and put him in his mobile home. I handed the mobile home to Nate. He held it at arm's length like our cockroach had cooties or something.

James Madison hissed.

"Don't take it personally," Tessa told Nate.

When they were gone, Tessa turned to me. "What next, Cammie?"

"I'm going to find Mr. Bryant and give Hooligan back. Then you and I are going to interview Mr. Schott—provided we can find him, that is."

What I told Tessa was true, but there was something I didn't mention. I wanted Granny's advice. I found her with Mr. Bryant in the Queens' Sitting Room.

Along with the Queens' Bedroom, it's basically Granny's apartment. They're at the east end of the second floor. The sitting room has blue-and-gold wallpaper and a tiny white marble fireplace.

Mr. Bryant was in an armchair with his e-reader. Hooligan circled twice and dropped to the rug. Mr. Bryant scratched Hooligan behind the ears.

"Granny, I need your help with the investigation," I said.

Granny looked me up and down. "Where's the bug?"

"Nate has him," I said.

"Proceed," she said.

"Tessa wants to question Courtney and then maybe her dad," I said. "I know Mr. Lozana writes mean things about Mom sometimes, but Courtney has been my best friend since second grade. If Tessa asks her questions, she's going to get all insulted and then she won't be my friend anymore."

Granny took off her glasses, rubbed her eyes and looked at me. "Cameron, you know you can't get to the truth if you let your feelings influence your detecting."

I looked at the carpet. "I know."

"So," said Granny, "do you think it's possible Mr. Lozana might have bugged your bug?"

"No!" I said.

"Really?" said Granny.

"Maybe," I said. "It turns out he was in the White House last night, and I can't figure out why."

"In that case, you have to treat him and Courtney just like all your other suspects."

I sighed. "I don't think I'm cut out to be a detective."

"You've done well on your other cases," Granny said. "I'd hate to see you give up now. Besides, a spy in the White House is a very dangerous thing. We have to get to the bottom of this, and soon."

Mr. Bryant cleared his throat. "If I may?" he said. "It's coincidental you should be talking about Mr. Lozana because just at this moment, I happen to be reading his blog."

Granny made a face. "I don't know why you give that blog the time of day, Willis. I have zero interest in anything Mr. Lozana writes."

Mr. Bryant said, "All right, then. I won't say one word more."

For a moment, the room was quiet.

Then Granny said, "Oh, fine. What did he write?"

Mr. Bryant started to smile, straightened it out, then read out loud: "'According to sources in the Parks White House, the president plans to add ground-up insects to school lunches at her earliest possible convenience. Yes, you read that right. Instead of being exterminated in school cafeterias, cockroaches may soon be on the menu.'"

"Oh, my stars in heaven!" Granny said. "Courtney must have reported what Mr. Amaro said at lunch yesterday to her father! But I thought we made it clear that the president is absolutely against it."

"Hooligan," I reminded her—and Hooligan thumped his tail.

"Ah, yes." Granny sighed. "Now I remember the

interruption. Does Mr. Lozana say anything else, Willis?"

"Only this," Mr. Bryant replied. "'Attempts to confirm details with Chef Amaro Amaro, a leading proponent of the bugs-for-food program, have thus far been unsuccessful.'"

"Wait a sec," I said. "Maybe that's what Mr. Lozana was doing at the White House last night, trying to interview Mr. Amaro."

Mr. Bryant nodded thoughtfully. "Perhaps."

"And something else, too," I said. "Mr. Lozana didn't know Mom was against the bug idea. But Tessa and I did. She told us so last night."

Mr. Bryant looked up. "Where was that?"

"Where did she tell us that, you mean? In our room. She came in to say good night after Granny did."

"Was your new pet listening?" Mr. Bryant asked.

I shrugged. "Sure, I guess. Like we already figured out, the spy must have put the tiny transmitter on him yesterday evening, so anything that happened in our room after that . . . Oh!"

Mr. Bryant smiled. "The spy heard what your mother said. Therefore, the spy knows bugs are not going to be on the lunch menu. Mr. Lozana, on the other hand, does not know this."

"Therefore, Mr. Lozana is not the spy!" I said. "My friendship with Courtney is saved! And that's not the only good thing."

"What else?" Granny asked.

"Basically, we've solved the case. I mean, we only have one suspect left."

Before I could tell them who that suspect was, there was a knock at the door.

"Excuse me, Judge, Mr. Bryant," said Charlotte. "But President Parks is requesting Cameron in the Oval Office for a meeting with Mr. Schott."

I jumped up. "Well, that's convenient! Thanks, Granny! Thanks, Mr. Bryant! You guys are the best!"

Granny nodded. "Aren't we, though?" Then she went back to her book.

CHAPTER TWENTY-FIVE

Charlotte and I stopped to pick up Tessa on our way. "Straighten your detecting cap," I told her. "You have a suspect to question in the Oval Office, and if I'm right, we're going to solve this case right now!"

Tessa jumped off the sofa. "What's Courtney doing in the Oval Office?"

"It's not Courtney," I said. "Mr. Lozana's not the spy." Then I explained about the blog post. "Hurry up!"

The kitten flyers were on Tessa's desk. She grabbed a stack on her way out the door. "While we're there, I'll post them for the people who work in the West Wing," she said.

"Seriously?" I said. "But you don't want to get rid of the Ks."

"I know, but it's like you said, Cammie. We can't win this fight."

This didn't sound like my sister, and I studied her

face for a second. Was I imagining it? Or was she trying hard not to smile?

To get to Mom's office from our bedroom, you go to the ground floor and hang a right. The West Wing is actually in a separate building, so you have to go outside on a covered walkway called a colonnade and pass the Rose Garden. Besides the Oval Office, where my mom works, the West Wing has offices for the vice president and some advisors, as well as a room for press conferences and space for the news guys.

Charlotte came with us. Most of the time, we're not allowed to leave the house part of the White House without either somebody from the family or somebody from the Secret Service.

Mom's secretary smiled when we got to the door and said, "Go right in."

The Oval Office really is oval-shaped. It has three tall windows with gold drapes, paintings of cowboy scenes on the walls and a bust of Benjamin Franklin on a table. George Washington's portrait is over the white fireplace. On the oval-shaped rug is a picture of the seal of the president of the United States. It has a gigantic eagle in the middle.

Since the room is a lot bigger than most offices, there's also space for sofas and comfy chairs.

Inside, we expected to see Mom sitting on one of the sofas across from Mr. Schott. What we never expected were two more people: Mr. Morgan and Mr. Webb!

"What are you guys doing here?" Tessa asked.

Mom frowned. "What my daughter meant to say was 'Good afternoon, gentlemen. How very nice to see you.'"

"That, too." Tessa nodded. "And Cammie and I are fine, just so you know."

"Glad to hear it," said Mr. Morgan. "To answer your question, we requested a meeting so we could report to your mother that the government sensing device is no longer detecting the AV signal from your pet cockroach."

Tessa and I looked at each other, then glanced sideways at Mr. Schott. I wasn't sure about my sister, but I didn't want to say anything about the investigation in front of our very last suspect!

Finally, I thought of a safe question. "Uh . . . what time did the signal disappear?"

Mr. Morgan looked at the notes in front of him. "At approximately thirteen-thirty-two today," he said.

"That's one-thirty-two in the afternoon," Tessa said. "We were outside in the Kitchen Garden. Maybe the signal couldn't be detected because James Madison was so far away."

Oh, Tessa. So much for not talking about the case in front of Mr. Schott.

Mr. Morgan asked, "Has the bug returned to the White House since then?"

Tessa said, "He's been back most of the afternoon."

"In that case," said Mr. Morgan, "it's most likely

that something happened to break the transmitter. Is that possible?"

Tessa and I looked at each other. "Hooligan."

Mom sighed. "Why am I not surprised?"

I explained how Hooligan had had to find James Madison, then fetch him from among the zucchini. "Maybe Hooligan bit the transmitter by mistake and broke it," I said.

"Or maybe dog slobber is toxic to technology," said Tessa.

Mr. Schott nodded solemnly. "Either is possible."

Tessa looked at Mr. Schott and crossed her arms over her chest. I got a bad feeling. She wouldn't try to question our last suspect right here in front of Mom and everybody, would she?

Yes, she would.

"Mr. Schott," my sister said, "how do you know that?"

Mom said, "Tessa!"

But Mr. Schott said, "Don't worry about it, Marilee. Among other things, my company makes government sensing devices, Tessa. That's why Mr. Morgan and Mr. Webb asked me here this afternoon. They needed some information, and I'm—*ahem*—an authority."

"Write that down, Cammie. He's an authority!" said Tessa. "Then tell us this, Mr. Schott. Why is it you were in Mr. Jackson's elevator last night? Isn't it true you were sneaking James Madison back into Cammie's and my bedroom so you could spy on us?"

Mom closed her eyes and silently counted to ten. She does this sometimes instead of screaming. "Tessa, your father and I have known Kirk Schott for twenty-five years," she said. "He has every US government security clearance there is. He is not spying on you."

Tessa waved her arms. "Well, I am sorry to have to tell you and the United States government that you're wrong, Mama. I know because we've eliminated all the other suspects!"

Mr. Schott's laugh creaked as if he didn't use it very often. "I was in Mr. Jackson's elevator last night because I had a headache and came back early from a reception."

Tessa said, "And do you have proof?"

Mom started to say something, but I was faster. "He's telling the truth, Tessa. He didn't do it, either."

Tessa waved her arms. "Again?"

"Think about it," I said. "The real spy didn't expect to get caught, right? So he must not have known that a government sensing device would detect the AV signal. Mr. Schott knows all about what government devices do. Therefore, he can't be the spy."

Tessa slumped down in her chair. "Oh, fine."

I was frustrated, too. But my brain kept right on working. I explained how the Hooligan alarm had sounded earlier and added, "If it was the spy who set it off, maybe he was going to our room hoping to find James Madison and fix the transmitter."

Mr. Morgan nodded. "That's a possibility, but there's another one as well. Now that he isn't transmitting, your pet is no longer useful to the spy. In fact, he poses a risk. If the transmitter is examined, it could be used as evidence."

I gulped. "You mean instead of wanting to fix the transmitter, the spy might have wanted to, uh . . . eliminate James Madison?"

Mr. Morgan nodded. "Indeed, Mr. Webb and I fear your pet is in very serious danger. From now on, if you hope to keep him safe, you must take every precaution."

CHAPTER TWENTY-SIX

A cockroach isn't cuddly.

A cockroach doesn't wag its tail.

A cockroach doesn't look up at you with love in its eyes, like Hooligan, or sing cheerful songs, like Humdinger, or lie on your feet to keep them warm at night, like the Ks.

But now that I'd known James Madison a while, I kind of liked him. His stripes were pretty. His antennae were graceful. And the spikes on his legs looked very punk.

Besides that, James Madison was our pet. If anything happened to hurt him, I'd feel terrible!

That's why, when we left Mom's office, I hurried back to warn Nate that James Madison was in danger. Meanwhile, Tessa said she'd meet the two of us at dinner. She had a stack of kitten flyers to post.

Mom and Aunt Jen both had meetings. Dad was in California building airplanes, which is his job during the week. He comes to Washington on weekends. Anyway, since they were all busy, Tessa, Nate and I were eating dinner with Granny in the Family Kitchen.

While Tessa and I folded napkins, we told Granny about our meeting in the Oval Office. Then Nate came in and set James Madison in his mobile home on the table. Granny crossed her arms over her chest, stared down at our cockroach and shook her head.

"But he's in terrible danger!" Tessa said. "We have to keep an eye on him at all times!"

"That doesn't mean he belongs on the dinner table," said Granny. "In fact, strange as it may seem, I prefer not to have cockroaches in the kitchen at all."

"Don't you love our pet cockroach, Granny?" Tessa asked.

Granny eyed James Madison through her glasses.

James Madison eyed Granny back.

"I would say I feel about him the same way he feels about me," Granny said after a moment. "But I will make you a deal. He can stay with us in the kitchen, provided he's out of sight."

Tessa closed James Madison in the drawer with the pot holders and dish towels. Then Granny served the plates. Her spaghetti and meatballs were delicious, as usual. We talked about protecting James Madison from the spy, and Granny told us her opinion: the only way to do it once and for all was to solve the case.

I looked at Tessa and Nate. "We know that, right?"

They nodded.

"The trouble is we're down to zero suspects," I said.

"What if you take the evening off?" Granny said. "You know how your muscles need to recover when they've worked hard. The same is true for your brain. Give it a rest, and tomorrow you'll come back smarter than ever."

"*Woot!*" Tessa surprised me by pumping her fist. "I know what we're gonna do tonight."

"What?" Nate and I asked at the same time.

"The best brain rest ever invented, duh—TV!"

Our TV is in the Solarium, which is at the top of the White House, connected to the third floor by a ramp. Besides the TV, there's a Ping-Pong table and also tons of windows. Outside, there's a balcony with a barbecue. Because it's so high up, there's a wonderful view of the city, especially the lights at night.

While Lily's parents were at their party, Lily had a babysitter. On our way upstairs, we stopped to ask if Lily could hang out with us till bedtime. Their family was staying in the Lincoln Bedroom, which is across the hall from the Queens' Bedroom—Granny's apartment.

In spite of the name, President Abraham Lincoln didn't ever sleep there, but he did use it as an office sometimes. Today it's decorated in old-timey style from the nineteenth century. The furniture is dark curvy wood with fancy carving on it, and the drapes are gold.

Honestly? I think it's ugly. Tessa, on the other hand, thinks it's perfect for a princess—meaning perfect for Tessa.

Anyway, the babysitter was glad to lend us Lily.

"What should we watch on TV?" Tessa asked her. "You're the expert."

"Pay-gown Smackdown!" Lily answered.

Of course.

Playground Smackdown is her dad's number one hit.

CHAPTER TWENTY-SEVEN

The idea of *Playground Smackdown,* in case you never saw it, is that grown-ups dress like little kids in shorts and T-shirts and race around an obstacle course that has teeter-totters, swing sets, monkey bars and a sandbox. To win, you have to be fast and coordinated, but you also have to use nasty tricks to stop your opponents.

Watching a lady in a Winnie-the-Pooh T-shirt pour molasses on a sliding board, Tessa said, "I'm an actual kid, but I would still be embarrassed to act like that on TV."

As you can imagine, Lily has seen every episode of *Playground Smackdown* about two hundred times. Now she pointed at the screen and giggled. "Watch dis pawt! I love dis pawt!"

I guess the camera was at sandbox level, because sneaker after gigantic sneaker pounded by, each one kicking up a dust storm that blotted out the sun. More exciting were the ants and caterpillars and earthworms. From that angle, they seemed as big as dinosaurs and twice as strange.

"*Ewwwww!*" chorused Lily and Nate.

Tessa said, "They're just misunderstood."

I didn't say anything. I was thinking about James Madison in the Kitchen Garden with mountain-sized zucchini.

Then I thought of something else.

When he was talking to Courtney and her dad, hadn't Mr. Verity said they used hidden cameras on his shows?

Maybe the camera Mr. Verity used for his reality show was the same kind as the one attached to James Madison.

While I was thinking, I spaced out the TV until a commercial made me pay attention. It was a promotion for the news with Jan and Larry.

". . . devil kittens at the White House," said the announcer. "Jan and Larry have the story at ten! Stay tuned!"

"Devil kittens—what?" I looked at my sister, who had clenched her teeth to keep from smiling. "Tessa—" I said sternly, but before I could say more Mrs. Verity—still in her glamorous clothes—appeared at the top of the Solarium's ramp.

"The party was a dud," she said. "So we're home early. And now, young lady, it's time for bed."

"No-o-o-o!" Lily protested.

Tessa was glad of the distraction. "How about if I come and read you a story?"

This worked like a charm. "Is that okay, Mommy?" Lily asked.

"Sure, and what a nice offer." Mrs. Verity reached for Lily's hand, and I noticed something for the first time. They were wearing matching nail polish—and it was orange.

"Piggyback!" said Lily.

"You're too big," said Tessa.

"I can take her." Nate bent down. "Hop on."

Lily climbed onto Nate's back, and they all headed toward the second floor.

"Come on, Cammie!" Lily called.

"In a second," I said.

The sight of that nail polish made me forget all about whatever it was Tessa was hiding. Wasn't nail polish an awful lot like paint? And maybe it wasn't only Mr. Schott who knew about technology.

I might be crazy.

But I might be on the brink of solving the Case of the Bug on the Run.

All I needed was one more thing: a trick question.

CHAPTER TWENTY-EIGHT

The next morning was Thursday, and we had to get up early. It was our California visitors' last day in Washington and—along with Mr. Amaro and Hooligan and Mr. Bryant—we were going to play tourist at the Lincoln Memorial.

Since the cats were still in not-so-solitary confinement down the hall, it was Granny who waked us. Apparently, the Bug Liberation Front protesters had taken the day off. Had they given up on freeing James Madison?

I hadn't told Tessa I had solved the mystery. I knew I might be wrong, and I didn't want to disappoint her again.

I didn't say anything to Nate, either. With him, if you're wrong, you will hear about it for the rest of your life.

So many people were going on our field trip that we had to take two vans on the mile-and-a-half drive. The Secret Service says it's a lot easier to keep us safe on the road than on the sidewalk, not to mention that we attract less attention.

Likewise, it's easier to keep us safe if we go places before they get crowded. That's why our vans pulled up to the bus zone behind the Lincoln Memorial at eight o'clock—a time in summer when sensible kids are still in bed.

Have you ever noticed that some ideas won't let you sleep? My idea about the identity of the spy was one of those. That's why I was yawning. And that's why—when I saw what I saw out the window—my first thought was that I had to be dreaming.

Then Tessa saw it, too. "What are they doing here, Cammie?"

It was the BLF! There were about a dozen people carrying signs, banging tambourines and chanting:

"I-N-S! E-C-T!
Every insect should be free!"

For a few minutes, we waited in the van on the street behind the memorial while Secret Service agents checked to make sure the area was safe. Then our driver got the all-clear, stepped out, came around and opened the door. One by one, we piled out of the air-conditioning and into the warm, sticky sunshine.

"I wonder how the BLF even knew we'd be here today," Nate said.

Tessa smacked her forehead. "I've got it! They're

the ones that have been listening to us! It's the Bug Liberation Front that bugged James Madison!"

Mr. Verity was standing beside us, adjusting the strap on his fanny pack. "Hey—Lily said something about a spy yesterday, right? So is that what she was talking about?"

I didn't know what to say, but Tessa never has that problem. "The First Kids have been investigating another mystery, Mr. Verity," she explained. "Someone was spying on us. Yesterday we ran out of suspects, but over there are twelve perfectly good new ones. Now that our brains are rested, we should interview them, Cammie."

"Uh . . . possibly, dear sister," I said, trying to sound as normal as possible. "But not till after our tour of the Lincoln Memorial."

"I think," said Granny, "that the BLF is here because the press is here. They have an amazing instinct for publicity."

Hooligan had been in his carrier in the back. Being a dog, he wouldn't be allowed on the tour. Instead, he was going for a walk with Mr. Bryant. We all hoped he would behave himself and no one would recognize him as anything more than a slightly funny-looking, too-energetic mutt.

"You know," Nate pointed out, "technically James Madison isn't a person, either. So he shouldn't be allowed on the tour."

"Wait—you've got the bug with you?" Mr. Verity asked.

"He's in his mobile home in the zipper pouch of my Barbie backpack," said Tessa.

"I don't think the Park Service will mind," Granny said, "provided he stays where he is."

Mr. Verity tapped his jaw with his finger. "You people," he said, "are too much!"

"Too much!" said Lily.

"Excuse me? Good morning!" A Park Service ranger waved to get our attention. "If you're all here, I'd like to get started."

The Lincoln Memorial is a big, old-fashioned temple made in a shape the Greeks used long ago, with plenty of white marble pillars around the outside. In the middle is a twenty-foot-tall statue of President Abraham Lincoln sitting on a chair that's more like a throne, if you ask me. On the walls are carved the words of two famous speeches he made. One of them is the Gettysburg Address, which begins, "Four score and seven years ago . . ."

Besides telling us about the building and the Civil War times when Lincoln was president, the ranger also told us a story about the statue. Some people think Lincoln's hands, resting on the arms of his chair, are forming his initials—"A" and "L"—in sign language. This could be because the sculptor had a deaf son, and Lincoln started a college for deaf people.

Or it could be that some people have too-energetic imaginations.

Our tour of the Lincoln Memorial took about half an hour.

When it was done, Mr. Verity, Nate, Tessa and I ended up standing next to each other on the steps overlooking the Reflecting Pool, and beyond it the Washington Monument; that's the tall skinny white one. A few feet away from us was a plaque marking the place where Dr. Martin Luther King, Jr., made his "I Have a Dream" speech about civil rights to thousands of people.

Because it was still pretty early, the only people we could see by the Reflecting Pool were Mr. Bryant and Hooligan, a park ranger on a mini-tractor, and the BLF protesters, with their signs and a tambourine.

Mr. Verity patted my shoulder. "Hey, Cammie, baby. Why the long face? Wassamatta U? Get it?"

"The boss means what's the matter with you?" said Max's voice from the phone clipped to Mr. Verity's belt. "The boss thinks he's hilarious."

"Because I *am* hilarious, buddy boy!" Mr. Verity said.

I tried to fix my face. "I'm okay."

But it wasn't true. I felt like an idiot. All through breakfast, the drive to the memorial and even the tour, I had been trying to think of a good trick question. But nothing sounded right. And if the spy figured out why I was asking, he'd lie and avoid my trap.

Not to be a drama queen like some people I could name (Tessa), but I was afraid that if that happened, we would never catch him, and James Madison would never be safe.

Standing on the steps, I was ready to give up.

Then Tessa asked me a question. "Did you feed James Madison this morning?"

And just like that, my problem was solved.

CHAPTER TWENTY-NINE

I spoke carefully. "I, uh . . . didn't feed him, dear sister. But don't you have some spicy taco chips in your bag? James Madison really likes those."

The phone on Mr. Verity's belt lit up. "Not the spicy ones!" said Max. "They'll upset his tummy!"

I turned toward Mr. Verity and saw his suntanned face turn almost as white as his teeth. Sounding exactly normal, I said, "Max, how do you know that?"

And Max said, "Uh . . . oops?"

And before he could say more, Mr. Verity grabbed the straps of Tessa's pink Barbie backpack, yanked it from her shoulders and ran.

Tessa was so surprised she didn't move for a moment. Then she slapped the place where her backpack used to be and shrieked, "Hey! You give that back!"

But by this time Mr. Verity was halfway down the memorial's marble steps.

"Come on!" I grabbed Nate with one hand and

Tessa with the other. "We've got to catch a bad guy . . . and save a cockroach!"

Together, the three of us gave chase, but Mr. Verity had longer legs and a head start. In a few more steps, he'd be on level ground, and then he'd have the whole National Mall ahead of him. Could I run two miles to save a cockroach? On a July day in Washington, I didn't want to have to find out.

Luckily, the Secret Service agents Malik and Jeremy were loping in our direction. And so were the BLF protesters, marching in time to their tambourine. That sound plus approaching sirens, Park Service loudspeakers and screaming tourists added up to a whole lot of noise.

Did I mention that Mr. Verity's run for it had also tripped the Hooligan alarm system? *"Awh-roohr!"*

Mr. Verity forged a zigzag path among the BLF protesters, but finally he busted free and beelined for the far end of the Reflecting Pool near the World War II Memorial. Jeremy and Malik were on their radios by now, alerting the combined forces of order to Mr. Verity's location so they could cut him off.

Tessa, Nate and I, meanwhile, fell farther and farther behind.

Then Mr. Amaro shouted: "Kids! Over here! I got me some awesome wheels!"

He was standing beside a green Park Service mini-tractor.

"Thanks!" Mr. Amaro told the ranger who had been driving. "I'll bring it back in no time."

The mini-tractor had a seat up front by the driver

and a bench seat in back. Nate, Tessa and I settled in, and Mr. Amaro gunned the motor.

"He lent you his tractor?" Nate had to holler to be heard.

"What can I say? He's a fan!" Mr. Amaro shouted back—and we sped toward the far end of the Reflecting Pool.

By this time a swarm of officers, tourists and news guys—not to mention one too-energetic dog—had Mr. Verity backed up against the pool's north rim. Brakes squealing, the mini-tractor jerked to a stop, and we all hopped off.

Mr. Verity was trapped, and he knew it. He looked right, looked left, looked over his shoulder . . . but there was no way out except to wade in.

I would have raised my hands in surrender, but not Mr. Verity.

He had one trick left. With a flourish, he pulled James Madison's mobile home from Tessa's backpack, then revealed what he was holding in his other hand—a spray can.

The crowd gasped. "Bug spray!"

Mr. Verity, who has probably seen every Clint Eastwood movie ever made, narrowed his eyes and snarled. "Do as I say and no bug gets hurt. Turn your backs, close your eyes, count to ten and then . . . say *adios* to me and the *cucaracha.*"

"Mr. Verity?" said Tessa. "May I just say one thing? That can you're holding? It's hairspray."

Mr. Verity hesitated just long enough to look at the

label. It wasn't much time, but it was enough. In a single bound, Hooligan performed a tricky leap-and-bump maneuver that knocked Mr. Verity back into the shallow water while at the same time jolting James Madison's mobile home free. Straight up into the air it flew, seeming to hang for a moment above the water.

Oh, no!

Madagascar hissing cockroaches can't swim!

Luckily, Aunt Jen played center field for her high school softball team. She jumped, she stretched, she reached . . . she gathered in the mobile home as if it were a high fly ball.

"Your cockroach, dear." She handed it to Tessa and made a face. *"Ewww."*

CHAPTER THIRTY

"Wait," said Courtney after lunch that same day, "does this mean my dad's not going to get his own reality-TV show?"

"Sorry," I said.

The two of us were in the Solarium with Hooligan. I was catching her up on our morning at the Lincoln Memorial.

"My dad's gonna be super-disappointed," said Courtney. "He was already shopping for houses in Hollywood. And was it really bug spray in the can?"

"It was," I said. "When Lily told Mr. Verity that she heard Tessa, Nate and me talking about spies, he knew he might be caught and bought bug spray just in case."

"I don't get it, though," said Courtney. "Why did Tessa say it was hairspray in the can?"

"To confuse him," I said. "And it worked, too."

Courtney shook her head. "Whoa—your little sister is smarter than she looks. But I still don't see how you knew Mr. Verity was the spy."

"It only came together after we'd eliminated all the other suspects," I said—leaving out the part where her dad had been one of them. "That's when I realized Mr. Verity could've been in our room when James Madison disappeared and again later when he came back. Plus, Mrs. Verity told us he was missing yesterday afternoon at the exact time somebody set off the Hooligan alarm in our room. Then, when we were watching *Playground Smackdown* last night, I figured out Mr. Verity knew the technical stuff the spy needed to know. Some of the cameras for his shows are miniature, same as the one the spy used on us. Finally, there was the orange nail polish."

"What shade of orange?" Courtney asked.

"Cockroach," I said. "We thought the spy must have painted the transmitter to hide it when it was attached to James Madison. Orange nail polish was perfect for the job, and the Verity family had a solid supply."

"That still didn't prove anything," Courtney said.

I nodded. "It was just a hunch. For proof, I needed a question. From listening in on Tessa and me, the spy knew certain things nobody else knew. If Mr. Verity let on that he knew one of those things, then he had to be the spy. When Tessa asked me about James Madison's breakfast, I remembered how we had talked about spicy taco chips being bad for cockroaches. Maybe Mr. Verity wouldn't have slipped, but Max did. He didn't want James Madison to have an upset tummy."

All this time, Hooligan had been sacked out motionless on the rug. Now he heard something, blinked and thumped his tail. When I looked, I saw Mr. Amaro coming up the ramp from the third floor.

"Hey, kids, I had an awesome visit to the White House, but this party's over and I am so, so gone!"

"I'm glad I had a chance to see you before you go," said Courtney. "My dad is really sorry he got it wrong about the bugs in lunches and everything."

"No skin off my nose," said Mr. Amaro. "I still think it's a genius idea, and if one of these days somebody wants to try it, I'll be the go-to guy."

"Are you taking the chef job in a certain nearby nation?" I asked.

Mr. Amaro shook his head. "Oh, man! You'll never guess! Turned out he wanted a personal chef for his dog! Not for me, chickadee. I'm headin' home to see the fam and rethink. No worries, though. When your name's Amaro Amaro, everything is awesome."

Solving the mystery and catching the spy made the First Kids pretty popular in the White House . . . at least for the rest of that day.

Tessa and I got a break from chores. Nate didn't have to practice piano. Granny even let the Ks out of not-so-solitary confinement. At dinnertime, we got our favorite: pizza from the White House kitchen, with blueberry ice cream for dessert.

Tessa and I were reading in bed when Mom came in to say good night. We hadn't seen her since we solved the case, but we knew she'd been briefed.

"Congratulations, muffins." She gave us each a kiss

and a snuggle. That felt great, but a few things had been bugging . . . er, I mean *bothering* me.

One was Lily.

"It must've been really hard for a little kid to see her dad arrested like that, wasn't it, Mom?" I asked.

"I don't think Lily saw what happened at the memorial," Mom said. "Kendall must have suspected something was wrong because she kept Lily far away from the action."

"What's going to happen to Mr. Verity?" Tessa asked.

Mom sat down on the edge of my bed and looked at her watch. "The family should be back in California by now. Next week, Ruben will have to return to Washington to go to court. He'll be charged with reckless endangerment of an insect and unlawfully attempting to dispose of a foreign invertebrate in a US government facility."

"What about spying on us?" Tessa asked.

"Ruben didn't do anything harmful with the information, so he'll probably get off with a fine," Mom said. "In fact, the news coverage of the standoff today caused ratings on all his reality shows to spike. I bet his company makes more money than ever."

"Well, that's not fair," said Tessa.

"I'm not saying he won't be sorry," Mom said. "For one thing, he will never be invited back to the White House. And for another, he has lost a good friend—me. It's a shame when money and fame make people think they can get away with bad behavior."

"I have another question, Mama," Tessa said. "Why did Mr. Verity want to spy on us in the first place?"

"I think I know," I said. "He wanted the First Kids for a reality TV show. We didn't know it, but we were auditioning."

Mom nodded. "That's about right. And you know something else? Even before the transmitter was broken, he knew the show wasn't going to work out. Not enough drama. Not enough humiliation. You guys are just too nice."

"Hmmph," said Tessa. "I think I am insulted."

"There is one other thing," Mom said. "Just what exactly is this? My staff has found them all over the West Wing."

Mom held up a sheet of paper—one of the flyers Tessa had made. It said: KITTENS FOR SALE. $100 EACH. Underneath was a picture of a black cat with sharp white teeth and fiery eyes. Surrounding the cat were stickers of ghosts and witches.

Tessa couldn't help it. She started to giggle.

The scary picture made me think of something else. "Tessa—are you responsible for the devil kitten story on the news last night, too?"

With an effort, Tessa straightened out her face. "Oh, fine. I confess. While Cammie was talking to Charlotte in the Kitchen Garden yesterday, I kind of told the news guys some stories about our kittens' evil behavior."

"What stories?" Mom said.

"You don't have to worry," Tessa said. "None of it was true."

"Oh, dear," Mom said.

Tessa shrugged. "I just want to keep the Ks. You can't blame me for that, can you? And anyway, you're always telling me to use my imagination."

"Can't we keep 'em, Mom?" I asked. "We have plenty of room."

"My job title says commander in chief," Mom said, "but it doesn't say a thing about kittens. You'll have to win over your grandmother."

"No problem. I have another idea," said Tessa.

"Oh, no," Mom and I said at the same time.

"It's nothing to worry about!" said Tessa. "Only . . . one of my friends from ballet has this really cool pet. It's a tarantula."

"Tessa . . ."

"So here's my idea. I promise Granny I won't ask for a tarantula, and she lets us keep the kittens. What do you think?"

WHITE HOUSE PROTESTS: ONE WAY THE PEOPLE TELL THEIR GOVERNMENT WHAT TO DO

In *The Case of the Bug on the Run,* an organization called the Bug Liberation Front (BLF) protests the First Kids' adoption of a pet cockroach because they believe insects should not be caged. The BLF is fictional, but real protests take place near the White House all the time.

For example, an animal-rights group called People for the Ethical Treatment of Animals (PETA) protested the White House Easter Egg Roll in 2012. Their idea was to call attention to the cramped and dirty conditions in which many chickens have to live. Instead of chicken eggs, the Easter Egg Roll ought to use plastic eggs, said PETA.

Why do people protest in front of the White House? For that matter, why do people protest at all?

Read on for the story.

POWER TO THE PEOPLE

The government of the United States of America is what's called a representative democracy. The word "democracy" comes from the language of ancient Greece, where *demos* meant "people" and *kratos* meant "power," so in other words, a democracy is a government in which the people have the power. The representative part means we don't have to vote every time someone wants to build a school, make a law or buy an aircraft carrier; instead, we go to the polls periodically to elect representatives who make those decisions on our behalf.

The president, who is elected every four years, is the most powerful and best-known of those representatives. Others include senators, congressmen and congresswomen, governors, mayors and school board members.

Government is just like any other enterprise. If the bosses don't know what they're doing, the enterprise is in trouble. Since the *people* are the bosses in a democracy, any person who wants good government should make it his or her business to understand how government works, what issues are important and what's going on in the country and the world.

People who go to the trouble to do that will probably want to express their opinions and, when necessary, work to make things better.

PROTEST LEADS TO CHANGE

Protest can be a step toward making things better. And if you want to attract the attention of the president, the members of Congress and the news media—or as Cammie Parks likes to call them, "the news guys"—then Washington, DC, is the place to go.

Among the many groups that have staged protests at the White House over the years are women demanding suffrage, the right to vote. These women were called suffragists, and they marched in front of the White House during Woodrow Wilson's second term as president, starting in 1916.

Wilson had never been a big fan of the vote for women, but at first he didn't mind the protesters. In fact, he often greeted them with a friendly wave. Then the United States entered World War I to oppose Germany, and the atmosphere became tense. One suffragist banner suggested Wilson was a hypocrite. In a speech, he had said he sympathized with the German people because they were not self-governed. The banner pointed out that American women were not self-governed, either.

In 1917, a few suffragist leaders were arrested and jailed for protesting in front of the White House. When some of the jailed leaders refused to eat, the guards force-fed them—making the news stories even more dramatic.

Wilson knew that press coverage of women being force-fed looked bad for his presidency. In 1918 he spoke out in favor of women voting, and in 1920 the Nineteenth Amendment to the Constitution was ratified, giving women the right to vote once and for all.

It wasn't protests by themselves that gave women the vote. For many decades, the forces of history had been moving toward that end. Still, the suffragists' White House protests did focus the attention of a nation . . . and a president.

CIVIL RIGHTS AND BEYOND

During the 1960s, protesters demanding civil rights for black Americans often gathered in Washington. The most famous of these gatherings was the March on Washington for Jobs and Freedom in 1963. As many as two hundred fifty thousand people came to the National Mall on August 28 to listen to songs and speeches. Among the performers were Joan Baez, Bob Dylan and Peter, Paul and Mary.

The speech everyone remembers, the one taught in the history books, was made by the president of the Southern Christian Leadership Conference, thirty-four-year-old Martin Luther King, Jr. In time it became known as the "I Have a Dream" speech. In *The Case of the Bug on the Run*, Cammie, Tessa and Nate stand on the Lincoln Memorial's steps very close to the spot where Reverend King stood.

An important White House protest for civil rights came almost two years later, in March 1965. That month, activists walking from Selma, Alabama, to the state capital, Montgomery, were stopped and attacked by local police. Their supporters gathered at Lafayette Park across Pennsylvania Avenue from the White House to demand that President Lyndon Johnson send federal soldiers to provide protection.

It was unusually cold that year, and some of the protesters huddled under blankets in the falling snow. The president paid attention, and on March 20, he ordered United States soldiers to go to Alabama.

Later in that decade and into the 1970s, protests targeted the increasingly unpopular Vietnam War. A banner unfurled on Pennsylvania Avenue in 1966 read: WE MOURN OUR SOLDIERS. THEY ARE DYING IN VAIN. In 1970, antiwar activists stacked thirty-seven cardboard boxes full of end-the-war petitions against the iron fence in front of the White House. Protests by some thirty-five thousand people on May 2, 1971, resulted in thousands of arrests and increased pressure on President Richard Nixon to end the war.

Over the years, the cause of peace has been promoted by antinuclear activists whose message is also proenvironment. In 1979 a serious accident at a nuclear power plant in Pennsylvania inspired some sixty-five thousand people to go to Washington to march near the Capitol and the White House.

Probably the most persistent protester in American history is Concepcion Picciotto, whose antinuclear peace vigil in Lafayette Park began in 1981 and, as of 2013, was still going on.

ALL KINDS OF CAUSES

While a protest over the fate of a single Madagascar hissing cockroach may be unlikely, it's true that all kinds of causes have drawn activists to the president's residence. In recent times, protests have called for action on gun control, abortion, the Israeli-Palestinian conflict, funding for AIDS research, gay rights and US support for the Baloch people of Pakistan.

In the spring of 2013, environmentalists and people worried about climate change protested a proposed pipeline to bring Canadian oil to refineries in the United States. Several were arrested after they tied themselves to the White House fence.

But wait a second.

If protesting is such a good thing, how come people are arrested for it?

The trouble is, protesters sometimes risk their own safety or get in the way of other citizens, like government employees, neighborhood residents and tourists. The suffragists arrested in 1917, for example, were convicted of obstructing the sidewalk and failure to disperse when told to do so by police.

Currently, there are regulations making it illegal for more than 750 people to demonstrate on the White House sidewalk. There are also limits on the size of protest signs, in part to ensure that tourists can take nice pictures of the White House. In 2011, a new law took effect that further restricts protests in places protected by the Secret Service.

Guess what happened after President Barack Obama signed that law?

Protests, of course!

CONSTITUTIONAL GUARANTEE

After the March 1965 protests, President Lyndon Johnson introduced important legislation to protect the voting rights of citizens regardless of race. Speaking to

Congress, he credited protesters with helping to bring about reforms:

"The real hero of this struggle is the American Negro. His actions and protests, his courage to risk safety and even to risk his life, have awakened the conscience of this nation. His demonstrations have been designed to call attention to injustice, designed to provoke change, designed to stir reform."

Whether the goal is civil rights, women's rights, animal rights or something else altogether, the government can't make improvements unless its bosses, the people, tell it what ought to be done. One way the people have done this throughout history is to protest in front of the White House.

If you want to know more about White House protests, a great source is the White House Historical Association, at www.whitehousehistory.org.